THE LONE TRAILBLAZER

SNEHA JAIN

*TO MY PARENTS , FOR MAKING ME BELIEVE IN MYSELF
WHEN NOBODY ELSE DID.*

Contents

Contents

Foreword

Dreams are the seedlings of reality. They sprout in the fertile grounds of our minds, watered by imagination and nourished by hope. This book, "The Lone Trailblazer," is not just a collection of words on pages; it is the manifestation of a journey that began with a single dream. Aadir, the protagonist of this story, embodies the spirit of those who dare to dream despite the odds. From the verdant fields of his village to the bustling streets of Mumbai, Aadir's journey is a testament to the transformative power of belief and perseverance. This narrative is a beacon for anyone who has ever felt like an outsider, for those who have been labeled as dreamers in a world that often values conformity over creativity. When I first conceived the idea for this novel, I was inspired by the countless individuals who, like Aadir, have walked the less-traveled path. Their stories of resilience and innovation compelled me to create a character who would resonate with readers across different walks of life. Aadir's story is one of triumph over adversity, of turning dreams into reality, and of the profound impact one individual can have on the world.

This book also pays homage to the mentors, friends, and communities that support dreamers on their journey. Through characters like Vadish,Paravi and the EcoInnovate collective, I wanted to highlight the importance of finding your tribe—those who see the potential within you even when you doubt yourself. Writing "The Lone Trailblazer" has been a journey in itself. It has been a process of self-discovery, reflection, and growth. Each chapter is infused with experiences drawn from my own life and the lives of those who have inspired me. The lessons embedded within these pages are universal: the importance of staying true to oneself, the power of resilience, and the beauty of daring to dream. As you turn the pages of this book, I hope you find a piece of yourself in Aadir's journey. May his story inspire you to pursue your own dreams with unwavering determination. Remember that being different is not a curse but a gift, and that within each of us lies the potential to create something extraordinary. To all the dreamers out there, this book is for you. May it serve as a reminder that the world needs your unique light, and that with belief, perseverance, and a little bit of magic, anything is possible. Welcome to the journey of Aadir, the lone trailblazer. May his story inspire you to blaze your own trail.

Warmest regards,
Sneha Jain

Preface

In the hushed anticipation before stepping onto the stage of the prestigious international conference, Aadir Mehta, now an elder statesman in the world of innovation and entrepreneurship, pauses behind the curtain. His mind drifts back to the humble beginnings of his journey, from the dusty streets of his small-town upbringing to the bustling metropolis where dreams are forged and tested. The tale I am about to share with you is not just a narrative of triumph over adversity; it is a testament to the power of resilience, the beauty of individuality, and the transformative potential of a single dream. Through the eyes of Aadir Mehta, our protagonist, we will embark on a journey that spans continents, decades, and the depths of the human spirit.

Dear reader,

As you embark on this journey with Aadir Mehta, may you find inspiration in his story, courage in his struggles, and hope in his triumphs. For in the tale of the lone trailblazer, we find echoes of our own journeys, and the reminder that within each of us lies the power to shape our destinies and change the world. With warmest regards,

Sneha Jain

Acknowledgements

Writing a novel is not a solitary endeavor; it is a collaborative effort fueled by the support and encouragement of countless individuals along the way. As I reflect on the completion of "The Lone Trailblazer," I am filled with gratitude for those who have contributed to its creation and brought its pages to life.

First and foremost, I would like to express my deepest gratitude to my family for their unwavering support and belief in my dreams. Their love, patience, and understanding have been my rock throughout this journey, providing me with the strength and inspiration to persevere in the face of adversity.

To my friends and mentors, thank you for your guidance, encouragement, and invaluable feedback. Your insights and perspective have shaped this story in ways I could never have imagined, and I am endlessly grateful for your generosity and wisdom. I am indebted to the few readers who dedicated their time and energy to providing feedback on early drafts of the novel. Your enthusiasm and constructive criticism have helped me refine and polish this story into its final form.

A heartfelt thank you to the publishing professionals who believed in this project and helped bring it to fruition. Your expertise, guidance, and tireless efforts have been instrumental in shaping this novel into a work of art that I am proud to share with the world. I would also like to acknowledge the individuals whose stories and experiences have inspired the characters and themes of this novel. Your resilience, courage, and creativity have left an indelible mark on me, and I am humbled to have had the opportunity to weave elements of your lives into this narrative.

Last but not least, I extend my deepest gratitude to the readers who have chosen to embark on this journey with me. Your curiosity, passion, and love for storytelling are the driving force behind my work, and I am honored to share this story with you. In the words of Aadir Mehta, the protagonist of *The Lone Trailblazer*," **Dreams**

are the seedlings of reality. "May this novel serve as a reminder that within each of us lies the power to dream, to create, and to change the world.

With heartfelt appreciation,
Sneha Jain

Prologue

In the quiet corners of the world, where the echoes of dreams linger in the air like whispers of forgotten promises, there exists a realm where the ordinary gives birth to the extraordinary, where the mundane transcends into the realm of magic. It is a place where the lone trailblazer roams, his footsteps leaving behind a legacy that defies the constraints of time and space. Our story begins in the heart of India, in a small town nestled amidst rolling hills and lush fields, where the sun rises with the promise of new beginnings and sets with the wisdom of ancient tales. Here, amid the dust and the din of everyday life, a young boy named Aadir Mehta first discovers the stirrings of a dream that would shape the course of his destiny. But Aadir is not like the other boys in his town. From a young age, he is drawn to the mysteries of the universe—the secrets that lie hidden in the stars, the wonders that await at the edge of the unknown. While his peers immerse themselves in the pursuits of youth—sports, games, and the simple pleasures of childhood—Aadir finds solace in the pages of books, where worlds beyond his imagination beckon with the promise of adventure. As the years pass and Aadir grows into adolescence, his love for learning only deepens. But with knowledge comes isolation, and Aadir finds himself drifting further and further from the world around him. His unconventional interests and insatiable curiosity set him apart from his peers, earning him the label of "the odd one out" among his classmates. Yet, amid the whispers of doubt and the shadows of loneliness, Aadir clings to his dreams with a tenacity that defies logic. For he knows that within the depths of his imagination lies the key to unlocking the mysteries of the universe, and that his journey has only just begun. And so, as the sun sets on the horizon and the stars begin to twinkle in the night sky, Aadir sets out on a quest to discover the true meaning of his existence. Little does he know that the path he has chosen will lead him to the very edge of possibility, where the boundaries between reality and fantasy blur and the dreams of a lone trailblazer become the stuff of legend. This is the story of Aadir Mehta, the boy who dared to dream, the man who defied the odds, and the trailblazer who changed the world. His journey is a testament to the power of belief, the strength of the human spirit, and the enduring legacy of those who dare to chase their dreams to the ends of the earth.

ONE

Aadir sat cross-legged on the floor, surrounded by a maze of wires and small components he had scavenged from old, discarded electronics. His room, a modest space with peeling paint and a single window overlooking the bustling street below, was his sanctuary. The broken radio lay in front of him, its insides exposed. He had spent the last hour meticulously examining its parts, trying to understand how it worked.

His father, Mr.Mehta, entered the room and watched silently for a moment, his heart swelling with pride. Aadir's curiosity reminded him of his own childhood, albeit with fewer resources.

"Aadir, what are you trying to do?" Mr.Mehta asked, kneeling beside him.

"I want to make it work again, Papa," Aadir replied, his eyes sparkling with determination.

Mr.Mehta smiled and picked up a loose wire. "Let me show you something." He began explaining the basic principles of circuits, and together, they spent the next few hours working on the radio. By nightfall, the room was filled with the soft hum of static as the radio crackled to life.

"You're a smart boy, Aadir," Mr.Mehta said, ruffling his son's hair. "Always remember, never stop questioning. That's how you'll learn and grow."

School was a battleground for Aadir. While his classmates chattered about the latest cricket match, he was lost in thoughts of science experiments and new books. During recess, he often found himself alone, flipping through his cherished science magazines or sketching diagrams in his notebook.

"Hey, Einstein!" a voice jeered, breaking his concentration. It was Ritul, the class bully, flanked by his friends. "What are you reading now? Trying to build a rocket?"

The other boys laughed, and Aadir felt his face flush. He wanted to retort, to defend his interests, but the words stuck in his throat. Instead, he closed his notebook and walked away, feeling the familiar sting of rejection.

That evening, at home, Aadir confided in his father. "Why don't they understand, Papa? Why can't I be like everyone else?"

Mr.Mehta looked at his son thoughtfully. "Being different is not a bad thing, Aadir. The world needs people who think differently. Your uniqueness is your strength. One day, they'll see."

Aadir shuffled home from school, his shoulders hunched and his face a mix of frustration and sadness. The jeers of his classmates echoed in his mind, their taunts about his love for science a constant reminder of his isolation. As he entered the house, his father, Mr.Mehta, noticed his son's despondent demeanor.

"What's wrong, Aadir?" Mr.Mehta asked, setting aside his newspaper. Aadir sighed, dropping his backpack on the floor. "It's just...the kids at school, they don't get me. They make fun of me because I love science. They think it's boring." Mr.Mehta looked thoughtfully at his son. He had always admired Aadir's curiosity and dedication, but he understood how hard it was for a child to feel different. "I think I know someone who might help," he said. "Come with me." Curiosity piqued, Aadir followed his father out of the house and down the street to a quaint, ivy-covered cottage.

Mr.Mehta knocked on the door, and it was soon opened by a petite, elderly woman with bright eyes and a warm smile. "Hello, Mrs. Iyer," Mr.Mehta greeted. "This is my son, Aadir. He's very passionate about science, and I thought he could learn a lot from you." Mrs. Iyer's face lit up. "Hello, Aadir. It's lovely to meet you. Come in, both of you." They stepped into a cozy living room, filled with bookshelves and the faint aroma of spices. Mrs. Iyer gestured for them to sit. "So, Aadir, I hear you love science. What's your favorite subject?" Aadir's eyes brightened at the question. "I love physics and astronomy, but really, I find all of it fascinating." Mrs. Iyer nodded approvingly. "That's wonderful. You know, science is like a never-ending adventure. There's always something new to discover. Would you like to see my collection of science books and equipment?" Aadir nodded eagerly, and Mrs. Iyer led him to a room that looked like a mini-laboratory.

There were microscopes, telescopes, beakers, and an array of scientific texts. Aadir's jaw dropped in awe. "Wow, this is amazing," he breathed. Mrs. Iyer chuckled. "I'm glad you think so. I spent many years teaching and collecting these. How about we start with a little experiment? Have you ever made a simple electric motor?" Aadir shook his head. "No, but I'd love to learn." Mrs. Iyer retrieved a few items and laid them out on the table. "It's quite simple. We'll use a battery, some wire, and a magnet. Watch closely." As she demonstrated, she explained the principles of electromagnetism in a way that was clear and engaging. Aadir followed along, his concentration intense. When they finished, he couldn't hide his excitement. "It works! This is so cool!" he exclaimed, watching the small motor spin. Mrs. Iyer smiled. "Science is full of these little wonders. And there's so much more to explore. If you'd like, you can come over after school, and we can work on different projects together." Aadir nodded enthusiastically. "I'd love that, Mrs. Iyer. Thank you."

Over the next few weeks, Aadir spent almost every afternoon at Mrs. Iyer's house. They delved into various experiments, from chemistry to biology, each session fueling Aadir's passion and confidence. Mrs. Iyer's encouragement and vast knowledge opened new horizons for him, and he began to feel less isolated. One afternoon, as they were packing up their latest project, Mrs. Iyer said, "You know, Aadir, being different isn't a bad thing. Your passion for science is something special. It can take you places you never imagined." Aadir nodded thoughtfully. "I just wish the kids at school understood that." "They might not understand now, but as you grow, you'll meet more people who share your interests. And who knows? Maybe you'll inspire some of them along the way," Mrs. Iyer said kindly. Aadir smiled, feeling a warmth in his chest. For the first time, he felt hopeful about his future. He knew he had a mentor who believed in him, and that made all the difference. As Aadir walked home that day, he held his head a little higher. The world seemed a bit brighter, and he felt ready to face whatever challenges came his way, knowing that he wasn't alone in his journey.

TWO

The science fair was the talk of the town, and Aadir was determined to make a mark.He went to Mrs. Iyer to show her his work.He sat at Mrs. Iyer's kitchen table, his notebook open and filled with sketches and notes. Mrs. Iyer hovered nearby, her eyes twinkling with excitement as she examined his latest idea. "So, Aadir, tell me more about your project," she said, leaning in to get a better look. Aadir grinned. "It's a water purification system. I read about how many people around the world don't have access to clean water, and I wanted to find a simple, low-cost solution.Therefore, I found a way to purify water through evaporation and condensation with solar energy." Mrs. Iyer nodded thoughtfully. "That's an excellent idea. How do you plan to make it work?" Aadir pointed to his drawings. "I'm using a glass partially filled with contaminated water,a clear plastic sheet to trap the heat of the sun,tubes for condesing the water and a collection vessel for purified water.I've tested it on dirty water from the pond, and it worked really well." Mrs. Iyer's face lit up with approval. "You're addressing a real-world problem with practical science. This is exactly the kind of project that will stand out at the science fair."

The science fair was only a week away, and Aadir poured every spare moment into perfecting his project. He faced constant jeers from his classmates, who found it more amusing to tease him than to understand his enthusiasm. "Look, it's Aadir the Water Boy!" Ritul sneered in the schoolyard. "What's next, solving world hunger?" Aadir forced a smile, but inside, the comments stung. He kept reminding himself of Mrs. Iyer's words and the importance of his project. Every day after school, he would head straight to Mrs. Iyer's house, where she helped him refine his presentation and offered endless encouragement. Finally, the day of the science fair arrived. The town hall buzzed with activity as students set up their displays. Aadir carefully arranged his water purification system, placing bottles of dirty water next to clear, clean samples that had been filtered through his system. He felt a mix of excitement and nerves as he looked around at the other projects, which ranged from volcanoes to solar systems. Just as he was making final adjustments, a group of his classmates approached, snickering. "Seriously, Aadir? Water purification? You think you're going to win with that?" one of them mocked. Aadir took a deep breath, trying to steady his nerves. "It's not about winning. It's about making a difference." They laughed and walked away, leaving Aadir to his thoughts. Just then, Mrs. Iyer appeared, a reassuring smile on her face. "How are you feeling, Aadir?" she asked. "Nervous," he admitted. "Everyone's making fun of me." Mrs. Iyer placed a comforting hand on his shoulder. "Remember, it's not about them. It's about the impact you can make. Trust in your work and believe in yourself."

As the judges made their rounds, Aadir explained his project with confidence. He demonstrated how the water purification system worked, showing them the before-and-after samples. The judges asked questions and demanded to see his water purification system working under the sun. Aadir took the entire set up outside and showed the judges its working, clearly impressed by the practicality and thoughtfulness of his solution. When the time came for the awards to be announced, Aadir stood among the crowd, his heart pounding. He listened as the third and second place winners were called, both for projects that were flashy and impressive. He felt a sinking feeling in his stomach, doubting his chances . "And now, the first place winner for this year's science fair," the announcer said, "goes to Aadir Mehta for his innovative water purification system!" Aadir's mouth dropped open in shock. Mrs. Iyer gave him a gentle nudge, and he stumbled forward to accept his ribbon and certificate. The applause was loud, and he noticed some of his classmates looking genuinely impressed. The announcer continued, "Aadir's project not only demonstrates scientific ingenuity but also addresses a critical global issue. His work is a reminder that science can be used to solve real-world problems." As he walked back to his display, his classmates approached him, their previous mockery replaced with curiosity.

"Hey, Aadir," one of them said, "that was actually pretty cool. How did you come up with the idea?" Aadir smiled, feeling a sense of validation and acceptance. "I just wanted to help people. There's a lot of science involved, but it's also about thinking how we can make the world better." Mrs. Iyer beamed with pride as she watched Aadir explain his project to his peers, his confidence shining through. As they packed up to leave, she turned to him. "You did wonderfully, Aadir. This is just the beginning for you." Aadir looked at his mentor, gratitude filling his eyes. "Thank you, Mrs. Iyer. I couldn't have done it without you." As they walked home, Aadir felt a new sense of belonging. He had found his place, not just in the world of science, but among his peers. His passion and hard work had paid off, and he knew that with Mrs. Iyer's guidance, there were no limits to what he could achieve.

THREE

The morning sun cast a warm glow over the Mehta household as Aadir sat at the breakfast table, staring at the letter in his hands. He was too surprised to blink.The crisp, official letterhead of St. Xavier's High School in Mumbai seemed almost surreal. Aadir's hands trembled as he opened it, reading the words over and over.He did not know that winning the science competition would land him an opportunity , this big. His father, Mr.Mehta sat across from him, his face a mix of pride and apprehension. "A scholarship to St. Xavier's, Aadir," Mr.Mehta said, his voice brimming with emotion. "This is an incredible opportunity. I'm so proud of you." Aadir looked up, his eyes reflecting a whirlpool of emotions. "I know, Papa. But it's so far away from home. I'll miss you and Mumma, and Mrs. Iyer too." Mr. Mehta reached across the table and placed a reassuring hand on his son's. "Change is always challenging, Aadir. But it's also a chance to grow. You've worked hard for this, and you deserve it. We'll always be here for you, no matter how far away you are." Aadir nodded, swallowing the lump in his throat. The excitement of the scholarship was tempered by the daunting prospect of leaving everything familiar behind.

That afternoon, he made his way to Mrs. Iyer's house, the letter clutched tightly in his hand. Mrs. Iyer welcomed him with her usual warm smile. "Come in, Aadir. What's that you have there?" Aadir handed her the letter, and she adjusted her glasses to read it. As her eyes scanned the words, her smile grew wider. "St. Xavier's! Aadir, this is wonderful news. I knew you had it in you." "But Mrs. Iyer," Aadir said hesitantly, "what if I don't fit in there? What if

I'm not ready?" Mrs. Iyer looked at him kindly. "It's natural to feel nervous about such a big change. But remember, it's your passion and curiosity that brought you here. Those qualities will help you succeed no matter where you go." She paused, then added, "And never forget, Aadir, that you're never truly alone. You carry the knowledge and support of everyone who believes in you." The days leading up to Aadir's departure were a whirlwind of preparations and farewells. His mother fussed over his packing, ensuring he had everything he needed. His father offered words of wisdom, reminding him to stay true to himself. And Mrs. Iyer gifted him a notebook, inscribed with a message: "For all your discoveries and dreams."

On the morning of his departure, Aadir stood at the entrance of his home, his suitcase by his side. The taxi that would take him to the train station idled nearby. He hugged his parents tightly, feeling a mixture of sadness and anticipation. "We're just a phone call away," his mother whispered, tears glistening in her eyes. Aadir nodded, taking a deep breath to steady himself. "I'll make you proud. I promise." The journey to Mumbai was long but filled with a growing sense of excitement. As the train sped through the changing landscapes, Aadir found himself daydreaming about his new school, the people he would meet, and the adventures that awaited him.

When the train finally pulled into Mumbai, the bustling city overwhelmed him with its energy and noise. He navigated through the crowded station, eventually arriving at the gates of St. Xavier's High School. The imposing, ivy-covered buildings stood tall, exuding an aura of history and prestige. Standing at the gates, Aadir took a moment to absorb the scene. Students milled about, their chatter and laughter a stark contrast to the quiet of his hometown. He felt a surge of determination rise within him. "This is it," he thought to himself. "A new beginning." A voice broke into his thoughts. "Hey, are you new here?" A tall boy with friendly eyes approached, offering a welcoming smile. "Yeah, I'm Aadir," he replied, extending his hand. "Just arrived from a small town." "I'm

Shourya" the boy said, shaking his hand firmly. "Welcome to St. Xavier's. You'll love it here. Let me show you around." As they walked through the campus, Shourya pointed out various buildings and shared stories about the school. Aadir felt his initial apprehension melt away, replaced by a growing sense of belonging. Later, as he unpacked in his dorm room, he found the notebook Mrs. Iyer had given him. He opened it to the first page and read her inscription again. Smiling, he picked up a pen and wrote his first entry:

"Day 1 at St. Xavier's. A new chapter begins. I am ready."

As the sun set over the city, Aadir stood by his window, looking out at the skyline. The future was uncertain, but he felt a deep sense of hope and determination. He knew he carried the support of his loved ones and the lessons he had learned with him. With that, he was ready to embrace whatever lay ahead. "Here's to new beginnings," he whispered to himself, a smile playing on his lips. "And to all the adventures that await."

FOUR

The morning air in Mumbai was humid, a stark contrast to the crisp, clear air of Aadir's hometown. As he walked through the gates of St. Xavier's High School, the buzz of the city seemed to seep into every corner of the campus. Students moved swiftly, their conversations a blend of English and Hindi, their clothes and gadgets reflecting the latest trends.

Aadir's first day began with a tour of the school led by Shourya.They walked through corridors lined with polished wood and glass, past classrooms equipped with state-of-the-art technology. Everything seemed so advanced and intimidating. "This is the science wing," Shourya explained, pointing to a row of doors. "We've got labs for biology, chemistry, physics—everything you'll need." Aadir nodded, trying to take it all in. "It's impressive. My old school didn't have anything like this." Shourya smiled. "You'll get used to it. Just remember, everyone here is passionate about learning. You'll fit right in." Despite Shourya's reassurance, Aadir found his first week challenging.

The curriculum at St. Xavier's was rigorous, far more advanced than what he was used to. In his first chemistry class, the teacher, Mr. Desai, quickly dived into complex concepts. "Today, we'll discuss the molecular structure of organic compounds," Mr. Desai announced. "Can anyone explain the concept of isomerism?" Aadir's hand hovered hesitantly, but several students' hands shot up instantly. Mr. Desai called on a girl in the front row. "Isomerism is the phenomenon where compounds have the same molecular formula but different structural arrangements," she explained confidently. Aadir scribbled notes furiously, feeling a pang of inadequacy. He had always been the top student in his old school, but here, he felt like he was constantly trying to catch up. During lunch, Aadir sat alone, observing his classmates. They seemed so polished, so at ease with each other. He overheard snippets of conversations about weekend plans, designer clothes, and the latest tech gadgets—things that felt foreign to him.

"Hey, Aadir, come sit with us!" Shourya called, waving him over to a table filled with students. Aadir hesitated but then picked up his tray and joined them. As he sat down, a boy with slicked-back hair and an expensive watch glanced at him. "So, Aadir, where are you from?" he asked. "A small town," Aadir replied, feeling self-conscious. "It's quite different from Mumbai." "I bet," the boy said, smirking slightly. "Must be a huge change for you." Shourya noticed Aadir's discomfort and quickly changed the subject. "Aadir's project on water purification won first place at his town's science fair. It's really impressive." The boy raised an eyebrow. "That's cool. We could use someone with your skills for the upcoming science competition." Aadir smiled gratefully at Shourya, feeling a little more at ease. After lunch, he headed to his next class, determined to prove himself. However, as the days went by, the challenges continued to mount. The pace of the lessons was relentless, and his classmates seemed effortlessly sophisticated, discussing topics he barely understood. One evening, feeling overwhelmed, Aadir called his parents. His mother's voice was a balm to his frayed nerves. "Mom, it's so hard here," he confessed. "Everyone's so smart and sophisticated. I feel out of place." "You're there because you deserve to be, Aadir," his mother said gently. "It's okay to struggle at first. Just keep doing your best, and things will get better." After the call, Aadir felt a bit more grounded.

He decided to visit Mrs. Iyer, who had given him so much encouragement before he left. He found her sitting in her garden, tending to her plants. "Aadir! How's St. Xavier's?" she asked, her eyes bright with curiosity. "It's tough, Mrs. Iyer," he admitted. "Everything's so advanced, and I feel like I'm always behind." Mrs.

Iyer patted the seat next to her. "Change is never easy, Aadir. But remember why you're there. Your passion for science and your determination got you this far. Use those strengths to overcome these challenges." She handed him a small plant. "Take this. It's a symbol of growth. Nurture it, and let it remind you of your own journey." Aadir took the plant, feeling a renewed sense of resolve.

Back at school, he threw himself into his studies with even more determination. He spent late nights in the library, catching up on topics he found difficult, and sought help from teachers and classmates whenever he needed it. Gradually, he started to find his footing. In biology class, he answered a question about cellular respiration with such clarity that his teacher, Ms. Fernandes, smiled approvingly. "Excellent, Aadir. It's clear you've been working hard," she said. Even his sophisticated classmates began to notice his efforts. During a group project, the boy with the expensive watch, Siddharth approached him. "You know, Aadir, you're pretty sharp. I was wrong about you," Siddharth admitted." Aadir felt a sense of accomplishment. He was still adjusting, but he was beginning to find his place. As the term progressed, Aadir continued to navigate the complexities of his new environment. There were still moments of doubt and struggle, but he reminded himself of Mrs. Iyer's words and the support of his family. One evening, standing by his dorm room window and looking out at the bustling city, he thought to himself, "I may be far from home, but I'm growing every day. This is just the beginning." With each passing day, Aadir's confidence grew, and he felt more determined than ever to succeed at St. Xavier's. The challenges were many, but so were the opportunities, and Aadir was ready to embrace them all.

Aadir's days at St. Xavier's quickly fell into a routine. Every morning, he woke up before dawn, quietly getting ready while his roommates still slept. The early hours were his favorite time to visit the library, a place of solace and knowledge. The smell of old books and the quiet hum of the air conditioning made it the perfect refuge. One morning, as he entered the library, the librarian, Mrs. Kapoor, gave him a knowing smile. "You're here early again, Aadir. Finding everything you need?" Aadir nodded, his eyes already scanning the shelves. "Yes, thank you, Mrs. Kapoor. I just want to make the most of my time." Mrs. Kapoor adjusted her glasses. "Your dedication is commendable. If you need any specific books or resources, don't hesitate to ask." "Thank you, I will," Aadir replied, heading to his usual spot by the window.

Hours flew by as Aadir buried himself in textbooks, trying to bridge the gaps in his knowledge. He often lost track of time, only realizing the hour when his stomach growled, reminding him to eat. The library became his sanctuary, a place where he could escape the pressures of fitting in and focus solely on his passion for learning. One afternoon, during a break between classes, Aadir sat alone at a table in the cafeteria, a biology textbook open in front of him. His classmates filled the room with laughter and chatter, but he remained engrossed in his studies. Shourya approached him, carrying his lunch tray. "Mind if I join you?" Aadir looked up, surprised but grateful. "Sure, go ahead." Shourya sat down and took a bite of his sandwich. "You know, you're always so focused. Don't you ever take a break?" Aadir shrugged. "There's a lot to catch up on. I don't want to fall behind." Shourya nodded. "I get it. But, sometimes, it's good to take a step back and relax. Why don't you come to the game night this Friday? It'll be fun, and you can meet more people." Aadir hesitated. "I'm not sure. I've never really been into games or social events." Shourya smiled awkwardly . "Just think about it. It might help you feel more at home here." Despite Shourya's invitation, Aadir found it hard to break out of his solitary habits. His evenings were spent much like his mornings—in the library or his dorm room, surrounded by books. His dedication began to pay off; his grades improved, and his teachers noticed his progress. In physics class, Mr. Shah announced a pop quiz. As the students groaned, Aadir felt a familiar twinge of anxiety. He took a deep breath and focused on the questions. When the results were handed back, Mr. Shah gave him a nod of approval. "Well done, Aadir. You've clearly been working hard." Aadir's face lit up with a rare smile. "Thank you, sir." However, his academic success didn't translate into social acceptance. His classmates respected his intelligence but found his solitary nature off-putting. In group projects, he often ended up doing most of the work himself, not out of necessity, but because he felt more comfortable relying on his own efforts.

FIVE

Aadir had started to make some efforts to socialize, he still felt a lingering sense of isolation. His life at the prestigious school seemed like a delicate balancing act between maintaining his academic success and trying to fit in.

One rainy afternoon, Aadir found himself once again in the library, poring over a particularly difficult physics problem. The rain pattered against the windows, creating a soothing rhythm that almost matched the pace of his thoughts. As he worked through the equations, he heard someone muttering nearby. "Ugh, this doesn't make any sense. How am I supposed to solve this?" Curious, Aadir looked up to see a boy about his age with curly hair and glasses, clearly frustrated with the textbook in front of him. Aadir recognized the look of confusion and felt an immediate kinship. "Having trouble with the physics assignment?" Aadir asked, approaching the boy. The boy looked up, surprised. "Yeah, it's the problem on quantum mechanics. I just can't wrap my head around it." Aadir smiled sympathetically. "Mind if I take a look? I've been working on the same assignment." The boy sighed with relief. "Please. I'm Vadish, by the way." "Aadir," he replied, sitting down next to Vadish. They spent the next hour working through the problem together, exchanging ideas and clarifying concepts.

Vadish had a keen mind and a deep curiosity, much like Aadir's own, and their combined efforts led to a breakthrough. "Thanks, Aadir. That makes so much more sense now," Vadish said, grinning. "I thought I was the only one struggling with this stuff." Aadir chuckled. "You're not alone. It's tough, but it's also fascinating once you get the hang of it."

As they packed up their books, Vadish asked, "Do you come here often? I've seen you around but never had the chance to talk." "Yeah, the library is my second home," Aadir admitted. "I find it easier to concentrate here." "Same here. Maybe we can study together more often? It's nice to have someone to bounce ideas off." Aadir agreed, feeling a warm sense of connection.

Over the next few weeks, the two boys became inseparable. They met regularly in the library, their study sessions filled with animated discussions about various scientific topics. Vadish shared Aadir's passion for science, and their mutual enthusiasm fueled their friendship.

One day, as they were packing up after a particularly productive session, Vadish turned to Aadir with an excited gleam in his eye. "I heard about this science competition coming up. It's a big deal, and the winners get to present their project at a national conference. What do you think? Should we enter?" Aadir's eyes lit up. "That sounds amazing. What kind of project were you thinking about?" Vadish pulled out a notebook filled with sketches and notes . "I've been working on an idea for a new type of renewable energy source. It's a bit ambitious, but with your help, I think we could pull it off." Aadir examined the sketches, impressed by Vadish's creativity. "This looks incredible. Let's do it." Over the next few weeks, Aadir and Vadish threw themselves into their project. They spent countless hours in the school's science lab, experimenting and refining their ideas. The project was challenging, but their combined skills and determination made progress steady and exciting. One evening, as they were working late in the lab, Vadish paused to look at Aadir. "You know, Aadir, I'm really glad we met. I've always felt like an outsider here, but working with you has made this place feel more like home." Aadir smiled, feeling a deep sense of gratitude. "I feel the same way, Vadish. It's been a long time since I've had a friend who understands me like you do."

As the competition approached, their project began to take shape. They designed a prototype for a renewable energy device that harnessed both solar and kinetic energy. It was an ambitious undertaking, but they believed in their work.

One day, while presenting their progress to their science teacher, Mr. Shah, they received some invaluable feedback. "This is impressive, boys," Mr. Shah said, looking over their work. "But remember, the judges will be looking for practical applications and real-world impact. Make sure to emphasize how your device can be implemented effectively." Taking Mr. Shah's advice to heart, Aadir and Vadish refined their presentation, focusing on the practicality and benefits of their invention. They practiced tirelessly, ensuring that every detail was perfect. Finally, the day of the competition arrived. The school auditorium buzzed with excitement as students from various schools set up their projects. Aadir and Vadish carefully arranged their display, nervous but determined. As the judges made their rounds, Aadir and Vadish presented their project with confidence. They explained the science behind their device, its potential applications, and its impact on sustainable energy solutions. The judges asked probing questions, and Aadir and Vadish answered with clarity and enthusiasm. After what felt like an eternity, the winners were announced.

"Third place goes to... Green Energy Solutions from Bright Future School. Second place goes to... The Robotics Team from Silver Oaks Academy. And the first place award goes to... Renewable Innovations by Aadir Mehta and Vadish Sharma from St. Xavier's High School!"

Aadir and Vadish stood in stunned silence for a moment before breaking into wide grins. They walked up to the stage to accept their award, the applause from their peers and teachers filling the auditorium. As they stepped off the stage, Shourya and several other classmates rushed to congratulate them. "You guys were amazing!" Shourya exclaimed. "That project was next-level." Aadir beamed. "Thanks, Shourya. It was a team effort." That evening, as they celebrated their victory, Vadish raised a toast. "To friendship and science. We make a great team, Aadir." "To friendship and science," Aadir echoed, feeling a sense of belonging and fulfillment he hadn't known before. In the days that followed, Aadir realized that his life at St. Xavier's had changed. He was no longer the solitary student struggling to find his place. With Vadish by his side, he had found a true friend who shared his passions and understood his challenges. Together, they had achieved something remarkable, and Aadir knew that this was just the beginning of their journey.

SIX

Victory at the science competition brought a whirlwind of change for Aadir and Vadish. No longer the quiet, studious boys at the back of the classroom, they were now the center of attention. The day after the competition, the school was abuzz with excitement. Students who had previously ignored them now approached with curiosity and admiration. "Hey, Aadir, that project was incredible," a classmate said during lunch, leaning over to get his attention. "How did you come up with the idea?" Aadir, who was still adjusting to the newfound attention, smiled modestly. "It was a team effort. Vadish and I brainstormed a lot before we landed on something that really worked."

Even Ruthvik, one of the more skeptical students, offered a grudging nod of respect when they passed in the hallway. "Nice job, you two," he said, his tone sincere if slightly reserved.

"Looks like we're not the lone wolves anymore," Vadish joked one day as they walked through the bustling corridors. His eyes sparkled with delight as he absorbed the recognition they were receiving. Aadir smiled back, feeling a warmth in his chest. "Yeah, it feels... different. But good." Their success opened doors they had never imagined. Invitations started pouring in for national science fairs, and local media picked up their story. They were interviewed by a local newspaper, and their photo appeared on the front page under the headline: "Young Innovators from St. Xavier's Make Waves."

One evening, as Aadir was deeply engrossed in a new physics textbook in his dorm room, he heard a knock on the door. It was the dorm supervisor with a letter in hand. "This just arrived for you, Aadir," he said with a smile. Aadir took the letter, noticing the official-looking seal on the envelope. He carefully opened it and began to read. His eyes widened with each line.

"Dear Aadir,

I came across your project on solar-powered water purification at the recent competition. Your innovative approach and dedication are commendable. I would like to invite you to join our summer research program at the Indian Institute of Science, Bangalore. It will be an excellent opportunity to further develop your skills and work with like-minded individuals.

Sincerely,

Dr. Radhika Sen"

Aadir read the letter twice, his excitement building with each word. This was an opportunity of a lifetime. He couldn't wait to share the news with Vadish. He grabbed his phone and dialed Vadish's number. "Vadish, you won't believe this!" he exclaimed as soon as Vadish answered. "We've been invited to a summer research program at the Indian Institute of Science in Bangalore!"

There was a brief moment of stunned silence before Vadish whooped with joy. "No way! This is amazing, Aadir. We're going places!"

As the news sank in, Aadir felt a profound sense of validation. All the late nights, the struggles to catch up, and the feelings of isolation now seemed to have a purpose. He wasn't just succeeding academically; he was being recognized by leaders in the field of science. In the following days, the excitement spread through the school. Teachers congratulated them, and even the principal called them into his office to commend their hard work and dedication. "This is a significant achievement for you both and for our school," the principal said, his eyes gleaming with pride. "You've set a great example for your peers. Keep up the excellent work."

As the summer approached, Aadir and Vadish prepared for their trip to Bangalore. They packed their bags with notebooks, textbooks, and all the essentials they thought they might need for the research program. The anticipation was palpable.

On the day of their departure, they wished that they had friends eho would come to see them off but they chose to focus on their journey ahead. The journey to Bangalore was filled with discussions about their hopes and aspirations. The Indian Institute of Science was renowned for its research, and the opportunity to work there was a dream come true.

As their train pulled into the city, Aadir looked out at the bustling metropolis, feeling a surge of determination. The campus of the Indian Institute of Science was even more impressive than Aadir had imagined. Lush green lawns, towering buildings, and state-of-the-art facilities surrounded them.

Dr. Radhika Sen herself met them on the first day, her presence commanding and inspiring. "Welcome, Aadir and Vadish," she said, shaking their hands. "I've read about your project, and I'm excited to see what you'll accomplish here. This program will be challenging, but I have no doubt that you're up to the task."

Over the next few weeks, Aadir and Vadish immersed themselves in their research. They worked alongside some of the brightest minds in the country, learning new techniques and expanding their understanding of environmental engineering. The experience was intense but incredibly rewarding. One evening, after a particularly productive day in the lab, Aadir and Vadish sat on a bench in the campus garden, reflecting on their journey. "You know, Aadir," Vadish said, looking up at the stars, "a few months ago, I never would have imagined we'd be here. It's all thanks to your determination and our teamwork." Aadir smiled, feeling a deep sense of gratitude. "We've come a long way, Vadish. And this is just the beginning. There's so much more we can achieve." Vadish nodded. "Absolutely. Here's to new horizons and endless possibilities." As they looked ahead, Aadir felt a renewed sense of purpose. The journey had been challenging, but with friendship and perseverance, they had turned their dreams into reality. The future was bright, and Aadir was ready to embrace every opportunity that came their way, knowing that he was no longer alone in his pursuit of knowledge and innovation.

SEVEN

Aadir stood at the gates of the Indian Institute of Technology, Mumbai, his heart pounding with a mix of anticipation and apprehension. The campus thrummed with activity, a vibrant tapestry of diverse individuals from all corners of the country. As he traversed the sprawling grounds, he couldn't help but marvel at the magnitude of the institution he was about to embark upon. The first week unfolded in a whirlwind of orientation sessions, introductions, and campus tours. The academic intensity hit Aadir like a tidal wave, catching him off guard with its sheer force. Professors wasted no time delving into complex subjects, leaving little room for hesitation or uncertainty.

In his inaugural engineering mechanics class, Aadir found himself drowning in a sea of equations and concepts. The sheer velocity at which information flew over his head left him feeling disoriented and overwhelmed. During the break, he mustered the courage to approach Professor Mehra, his voice tinged with uncertainty. "Excuse me, sir," Aadir began tentatively. "I'm finding the material a bit overwhelming. Could you recommend any resources to help me catch up?" Professor Mehra regarded him with a mixture of surprise and empathy. "It's not uncommon to feel this way, especially in the beginning," he reassured Aadir. "Focus on grasping the fundamentals. The library is an invaluable resource, and I'm here to provide guidance whenever you need it." Gratitude washed over Aadir as he nodded, his determination flickering to life within him. "Thank you, sir. I'll make sure to do that."

That evening, Aadir found solace amidst the towering shelves of the library, his determination propelling him forward. Armed with textbooks and online lectures, he delved into the intricate world of engineering mechanics, each page a testament to his unwavering resolve. As the days turned into weeks, Aadir found himself navigating the intricate web of academic rigor and cultural diversity that defined life at IIT Mumbai. He attended lectures, engaged in group study sessions, and forged connections with students from every corner of the nation. During a break between classes, Aadir found himself in the cafeteria, surrounded by a cacophony of languages and laughter.

Nearby, a group of students engaged in animated discussion about a particularly challenging problem from their thermodynamics class. "Mind if we join you?" Aadir asked, approaching the group with a tentative smile. "Of course, come on over," one of the students replied warmly. "I'm Paravi. You guys must be new here." "Aadir and Vadish," Aadir introduced himself and Vadish, feeling a sense of camaraderie settle over him. "Yeah, it's our first week. The pace here is quite intense." Paravi nodded sympathetically, her eyes sparkling with understanding. "It can be overwhelming, but you'll find your rhythm soon enough. And remember, we're all in this together."

As the semester progressed, Aadir found himself navigating the peaks and valleys of his newfound journey with Vadish by his side. Together, they weathered the storms of uncertainty and celebrated the triumphs of perseverance. With each passing day, Aadir grew more resilient, his spirit fortified by the knowledge that he wasn't alone in his struggles. As he embraced the vibrant tapestry of experiences that awaited him at IIT Mumbai, he knew that he was embarking on a journey that would shape him in ways he had never dared to dream.

The study group meetings with Paravi became a cornerstone of Aadir's academic journey at IIT. Surrounded by peers who shared his passion for learning, he found himself thriving in the intellectual environment. The discussions sparked new ideas and perspectives, igniting a fire within him that had long lay dormant. One day, as he sat in a lecture on renewable energy, Aadir's mind wandered, exploring the possibilities beyond the confines of the classroom.

Suddenly, inspiration struck like a bolt of lightning. He envisioned a device that could harness kinetic energy from everyday activities, such as walking or cycling, to generate electricity. Eager to explore this newfound idea, he excused himself from the lecture and hurried to the library to delve deeper into the concept. Over the following weeks, Aadir threw himself into his work with unwavering dedication. He spent countless hours in the lab, meticulously crafting his prototype from scratch. Late nights blurred into early mornings as he fine-tuned every detail, driven by a burning desire to bring his vision to life. His efforts did not go unnoticed. Professor Mehra, impressed by Aadir's innovative spirit, took notice of his relentless pursuit of excellence. During one of their office hours, he invited Aadir to share more about his project. "Tell me more about your project, Aadir," Professor Mehra said, his eyes gleaming with curiosity. Aadir eagerly launched into an animated explanation, his passion evident in every word. He described the design, the materials, and the potential applications of his device, his excitement palpable. Professor Mehra listened intently, nodding along as Aadir spoke.

When he had finished, the professor leaned back in his chair, a thoughtful expression on his face. "This is truly remarkable, Aadir. Your ingenuity and creativity are commendable. I believe this project has the potential to make a significant impact." A surge of pride swelled within Aadir at the professor's words. To have his idea recognized and validated by someone of Mehra's stature was a momentous milestone. But it was the professor's next words that truly took his breath away. "I would like to mentor you on this project," Professor Mehra said, his voice filled with genuine enthusiasm. "Together, we can refine your prototype, explore new avenues, and push the boundaries of innovation." Aadir's heart raced with excitement at the prospect of working alongside

Professor Mehra, a respected authority in the field. With his guidance and expertise, he knew that the possibilities were limitless.

Under Professor Mehra's mentorship, Aadir delved deeper into his project, pushing the boundaries of what was thought possible. They explored advanced materials, experimented with cutting-edge technologies, and fine-tuned every aspect of the prototype to perfection. As the weeks turned into months, Aadir's project gained momentum, drawing attention from his peers and professors alike. His confidence soared, bolstered by the unwavering support of his mentor and the validation of his peers. The journey was not without its challenges, but with each obstacle they encountered, Aadir and Professor Mehra emerged stronger and more determined than ever. Together, they forged ahead, driven by a shared vision of innovation and excellence. And as Aadir stood on the precipice of a new era of discovery, he knew that this was only the beginning of what promised to be an extraordinary journey filled with endless possibilities.

EIGHT

The demands of college life weighed heavily on Aadir's shoulders. Balancing his academics, innovative project, and personal life seemed like an insurmountable challenge. Days blurred into nights as he juggled coursework, project development, and study group meetings, often sacrificing sleep and personal time in the relentless pursuit of success. His friends began to notice the toll it was taking on him.

One evening, as they gathered in their dorm room, Vadish couldn't help but comment on Aadir's appearance. "Aadir, you look exhausted," he remarked, concern evident in his voice as he observed the dark circles under Aadir's eyes. "You need to take a break." "I can't, Vadish," Aadir replied, his voice strained with fatigue and determination. "There's too much to do. I can't afford to fall behind." Despite his best efforts, the mounting pressure began to take its toll on Aadir. He missed deadlines, struggled with assignments, and felt a growing sense of inadequacy gnawing at his confidence. His once vibrant friendships also began to suffer as he became increasingly irritable and withdrawn, his focus consumed by the relentless pursuit of academic excellence. One night, after a particularly stressful day, Aadir found himself alone in the empty library, his head in his hands as he grappled with overwhelming feelings of exhaustion and despair. It felt as though the weight of the world was bearing down on him, threatening to crush him under its relentless pressure.

It was then that Paravi, one of his closest friends, found him. Her expression softened with concern as she approached him, her voice gentle yet firm. "Aadir, you can't keep pushing yourself like this. It's okay to ask for help." Her words struck a chord deep within Aadir's soul. For the first time in a long while, he allowed himself to acknowledge the extent of his struggles. He realized that he couldn't continue down this path of self-destruction indefinitely. Summoning his courage, Aadir sought guidance from Professor Mehra, his mentor and confidant. In their meeting, he poured out his heart, sharing the overwhelming pressures he faced and the toll it was taking on his well-being.

Professor Mehra listened attentively, his expression one of empathy and understanding. "Aadir, success isn't just about hard work," he reminded him gently. "It's also about balance. Take time to rest and recharge. Your well-being is just as important as your achievements." Those words resonated deeply with Aadir, serving as a poignant reminder of the importance of self-care and resilience in the face of adversity. With the professor's sage advice as his guiding light, Aadir embarked on a journey of self-discovery and healing. He began to incorporate regular breaks into his schedule, prioritizing moments of rest and relaxation amidst the relentless demands of college life. He practiced mindfulness and sought solace in the support of his friends, finding strength in their unwavering presence by his side. Gradually, Aadir began to find a better balance between his academic pursuits and his personal well-being. Though the journey was fraught with challenges and setbacks, he emerged stronger and more resilient than ever before, ready to face whatever obstacles lay ahead with renewed vigor and determination.

NINE

v With newfound clarity and determination, Aadir embraced a fresh approach to managing his time and stress. His days were meticulously organized, each moment optimized for maximum efficiency. As a result, he found himself more focused and productive than ever before, excelling in his studies and project alike. His efforts did not go unnoticed.

Aadir's exemplary performance in his exams garnered praise from his professors, his grades reflecting the fruits of his labor and dedication. Meanwhile, his project on kinetic energy harvesting gained momentum, drawing interest from fac vulty and peers alike. One day, as Aadir stood before a panel of professors, presenting his refined prototype, he received an unexpected visitor: Dr. Sen, the renowned scientist who had played a pivotal role in shaping his journey.

"Impressive work, Aadir," Dr. Sen remarked, his eyes alight with admiration as he examined the intricate details of the device. "Your innovation could have significant implications for sustainable energy solutions." A surge of pride coursed through Aadir's veins at the esteemed scientist's words. "Thank you, Dr. Sen. Your guidance and support have been invaluable in bringing this project to fruition." Dr. Sen smiled warmly, his expression one of genuine pride. "I have another opportunity for you, Aadir. The International Conference on Renewable Energy is being held in Singapore next month. I would like you to present your work there. It's a prestigious platform and could open many doors for you."

Aadir's heart skipped a beat at the unexpected invitation. An international conference was the culmination of a lifelong dream, a chance to showcase his work on a global stage. "I... I don't know what to say. Thank you, Dr. Sen. I would be honored." As he shared the news with his friends and mentors, Aadir felt a profound sense of accomplishment wash over him. The struggles and sacrifices of the past were but stepping stones on the path to this moment. He was on the cusp of a new beginning, ready to share his work with the world and embark on the next chapter of his extraordinary journey.

Preparation for the international conference consumed Aadir's days and nights. With unwavering determination, he poured over every detail of his presentation, meticulously perfecting each slide, and rehearsing his speech until it flowed effortlessly from his lips. The support he received from his mentors and friends proved invaluable, guiding him through the intricate process with unwavering patience and encouragement. "Clarity and confidence, Aadir," Professor Mehra reminded him during one of their practice sessions, his voice a steady anchor amidst the storm of nerves that threatened to overwhelm Aadir. "Explain your concept in simple terms and let your passion shine through."

Vadish and Paravi were by his side every step of the way, offering their expertise in visual design and presentation flow. "You've got this, Aadir," Vadish reassured him, his unwavering belief bolstering Aadir's resolve. "Just be yourself." On the day of the conference, Aadir's heart raced with anticipation as he stepped into the grand venue, his senses inundated by the sight of renowned scientists, researchers, and industry leaders milling about. The air buzzed with excitement and anticipation, a palpable energy that fueled Aadir's determination to make his mark on the world stage. As he waited for his turn to present, Aadir found solace in the memories of his journey—the obstacles he had overcome, the lessons he had learned, and the unwavering support of those who had stood by his side through it all. With each passing moment, his nerves gave way to a quiet confidence, a steadfast belief in the value of his work and the impact it could have on the world. When his name was called, Aadir took a deep breath and stepped onto the stage, the spotlight casting a warm glow around him.

His hands trembled slightly as he adjusted the microphone, but as he looked out at the sea of expectant faces, a calm certainty settled over him like a comforting embrace. He began his presentation, his voice steady and clear as he walked the audience through the intricacies of his project. With each slide, each word, he felt the weight of his journey lifting from his shoulders, replaced by a sense of purpose and pride that filled him with a quiet resolve. The audience listened intently, captivated by Aadir's passion and expertise. As he demonstrated his prototype, he saw heads nodding in understanding and appreciation. When he finished, the room erupted in applause, a symphony of validation that reverberated through his soul. The Q&A session that followed was challenging but invigorating, with questions probing the depths of his research and the potential applications of his innovation.

Aadir fielded each inquiry with grace and poise, his confidence buoyed by the knowledge that he had earned his place on the international stage. As he stepped off the stage, he was met with a proud smile from Dr. Sen, whose unwavering support had been a guiding light throughout his journey. "Well done, Aadir," she said, her voice filled with genuine pride. "You've made a significant impression today." Aadir felt a swell of emotion rise within him—a sense of accomplishment and gratitude that transcended words. This was not just a personal victory but a testament to the support and guidance he had received along the way. As he mingled with the crowd, exchanging ideas and forging connections, he knew that this was only the beginning of a new chapter in his journey—one filled with endless possibilities and opportunities for growth and discovery.

TEN

Returning from the international conference, Aadir was filled with a renewed sense of purpose. His mind buzzed with the possibilities his innovation could unlock. One evening, he gathered his closest friends, Vadish and Paravi, at a cozy cafe in Mumbai to share his vision. "We need to take the next step," Aadir began, his eyes shining with excitement. "I believe we can create a company dedicated to sustainable energy solutions. We can make a real difference." Vadish leaned back in his chair, considering. "It's a big leap, Aadir. Starting a business is no small feat." Paravi nodded in agreement. "But it's also an incredible opportunity. We've seen the potential of your idea. I'm in." Aadir's face broke into a smile. "Great! I've been thinking about a name—'EcoInnovate.' What do you think?" "Perfect," Paravi said. "It captures the essence of what we want to achieve."

Their first major task was to secure funding. Aadir and Paravi spent countless hours preparing a comprehensive business plan, detailing their vision, market analysis, and financial projections. They pitched to numerous investors, facing more rejections than they cared to count. During one particularly discouraging meeting, an investor dismissed their idea with a wave of his hand. "This is too ambitious for a startup. Come back when you have something more concrete." As they left the office, Aadir felt a wave of frustration. "Maybe we're aiming too high," he said, slumping against a wall. Paravi put a hand on his shoulder. "We just haven't found the right investor yet. Let's keep going." Their persistence finally paid off when they met Mr. Desai, a prominent angel investor known for his interest in sustainable technologies. During their pitch, he listened intently, occasionally nodding as Aadir outlined their plan. After a thoughtful pause, Mr. Desai spoke. "I see potential in your idea. I'm willing to fund your startup." Aadir could hardly believe it. "Thank you, Mr. Desai. We won't let you down." With funding secured, they rented a small office in the bustling heart of Mumbai.

The space was modest, but to them, it was a sanctuary of innovation and potential. They divided the responsibilities: Vadish focused on the technical development, Paravi managed the operations and logistics, and Aadir oversaw the strategy and vision. The initial days were a whirlwind of activity. They encountered numerous challenges—from technical glitches in the prototype to supply chain issues. One night, as they were working late in the office, Vadish sighed in frustration. "The prototype keeps overheating. We're missing something." Aadir moved over to Vadish's workstation, peering at the schematics. "Let's look at the cooling system again. Maybe there's a more efficient design we can implement." Their collaborative efforts paid off. After days of trial and error, they successfully created a working prototype. The team celebrated this milestone with a modest but heartfelt toast in their office. "To EcoInnovate!" Aadir said, raising his glass of soda. "And to our future." Despite the long hours and mounting stress, their shared sense of purpose kept them motivated. They celebrated every small victory, from securing a patent to their first successful test run. One afternoon, as they were finalizing plans for their first public demonstration, Paravi looked around the room at her friends. "We've come a long way. Remember when we were just three students with a dream?" Aadir smiled, feeling a deep sense of pride and gratitude. "And now we're turning that dream into reality. This is just the beginning." As the chapter of their startup unfolded, they faced each challenge with resilience, driven by their vision of a sustainable future. And with each step forward, Aadir felt more confident in their mission and more certain that they were on the brink of something extraordinary.

With the initial success of EcoInnovate, Aadir and his team found themselves facing the daunting task of scaling up their operations. Orders for their energy-efficient device poured in from across the country, far exceeding their current production capacity. To meet this growing demand, they partnered with a larger manufacturing facility. However, this brought a host of new challenges. As Aadir walked through the sprawling manufacturing floor of their new partner, he felt a mix of excitement and anxiety. The scale of operations here was immense compared to their modest setup. He met with the plant manager, Mr. Patel, to discuss the production plan. "We'll need to ensure that quality control remains our top priority," Aadir said firmly. "Our customers trust us for reliable and high-quality products." Mr. Patel nodded. "Absolutely, Aadir. We'll implement a dedicated quality control team for your production line. But be aware, scaling up quickly can sometimes lead to hiccups." True to his word, the initial batches from the new facility faced several issues. There were delays in delivery, and some products had minor defects. Customer complaints started trickling in, causing Aadir sleepless nights. One evening, as the team gathered in their office, the tension was palpable.

Paravi, usually calm, was visibly frustrated. "We need to fix these supply chain issues, Aadir. We can't afford to lose our customers' trust." Vadish, who had been reviewing the production reports, added, "And we need more stringent quality control measures. These defects are unacceptable." Aadir took a deep breath. "I agree with both of you. Let's divide and conquer. Paravi, focus on the supply chain. Work with our suppliers to ensure timely delivery of materials. Vadish, oversee the quality control processes at the manufacturing plant. I'll handle customer communications and ensure we manage their expectations." --- Paravi threw herself into improving the supply chain. She visited suppliers, negotiated better terms, and implemented a more robust tracking system. This helped reduce delays and ensured a steady flow of materials to the manufacturing plant.

Meanwhile, Vadish worked closely with Mr. Patel's team, setting up rigorous quality control protocols. They identified the root causes of the defects and made necessary adjustments to the production line. Weekly quality audits became mandatory, and any defective items were immediately rectified. Despite their efforts, internal tensions began to surface. The workload was overwhelming, and stress levels were high. Paravi and Vadish, both passionate and driven, often clashed over priorities. During one heated discussion, Paravi exclaimed, "We can't just focus on fixing defects, Vadish. We need to prevent them in the first place!" Vadish shot back, "And we can't prevent them if we don't understand why they're happening! We need to focus on thorough testing."

Aadir, sensing the need to mediate, stepped in. "Both of you are right. Prevention and testing are equally important. Let's work together to create a balanced approach. Open communication is key. We're a team, and we need to act like one." To foster better teamwork, Aadir introduced regular strategy meetings where everyone could voice their concerns and suggest solutions. These meetings helped clear misunderstandings and aligned their efforts towards common goals.

Slowly but surely, their hard work began to pay off. The supply chain stabilized, quality control improved, and customer satisfaction levels rose. They hired additional staff to manage the increased workload and invested in new technologies to enhance efficiency.

One afternoon, as the team gathered to review their progress, Aadir felt a sense of accomplishment. "We've come a long way," he said, looking around at his friends and colleagues. "We faced many challenges, but we tackled them head-on and emerged stronger." Paravi smiled. "It hasn't been easy, but we've learned a lot. We're more resilient now." Vadish added, "And we're better prepared for the future. Whatever comes next, we'll handle it together." Their journey had been fraught with challenges, but they had navigated through them with determination and teamwork. The lessons learned during this phase were invaluable, preparing them for the next steps in their entrepreneurial adventure. As they toasted to their achievements with cups of chai, Aadir couldn't help but feel grateful. They had managed to stabilize operations, meet customer demands, and maintain product quality. But most importantly, they had grown as a team, ready to face whatever the future held. EcoInnovate was no longer just a startup; it was a testament to their resilience and a beacon of innovation in the field of sustainable energy. And as they looked towards the future, Aadir knew that this was just the beginning of their remarkable journey.

ELEVEN

EcoInnovate's innovative approach to sustainable energy solutions began to garner national recognition. Their success story was featured in several prestigious magazines and news outlets, and they were invited to speak at numerous conferences and workshops. The crowning achievement was when EcoInnovate won the National Green Innovation Award, a testament to their hard work and dedication. As Aadir stood at the podium to receive the award, he couldn't help but feel a surge of pride. He looked out at the audience, filled with industry leaders and innovators, and began his acceptance speech. "This award is not just a recognition of our product," Aadir said, "but of the collective effort of our team and the belief that sustainable innovation can change the world." The applause was thunderous, and for a moment, it felt like all their struggles had been worth it.

The next morning, Aadir was preparing for a television interview when his phone rang. It was Vadish, and his voice was filled with panic. "We've got a problem. One of our latest batches has a major defect. Customers are reporting failures." Aadir's heart sank. "How bad is it?" "Bad. We need to recall the batch and fix the issue immediately." The next few weeks were a blur of frantic activity. The team worked around the clock to identify the root cause of the defect, recall the faulty products, and reassure their customers. It was a costly setback, both financially and reputationally. Aadir felt the weight of responsibility pressing down on him, but the unwavering support of his team kept him going. Paravi and Vadish took charge of the technical investigation. They discovered that a supplier had provided substandard components, leading to the failures.

Paravi coordinated with the supplier to ensure better quality control, while Vadish implemented additional testing protocols to prevent future issues. "We need to restore our customers' trust," Aadir said during one of their emergency meetings. "Let's offer free replacements and extended warranties for those affected." The recall process was grueling, but the team's swift response and transparent communication helped mitigate the damage. Slowly, customer confidence began to rebuild. --- Just as EcoInnovate was starting to recover, they were hit with another blow. A legal notice arrived from a competitor, accusing them of patent infringement. The lawsuit threatened to derail their progress and drain their resources. "This is ridiculous," Paravi said, reviewing the legal documents with a furrowed brow. "We didn't infringe on any patents. This is a baseless claim."

Aadir knew they couldn't let the lawsuit go unanswered. They hired a legal team and began gathering evidence to defend their position. The legal battle was stressful and time-consuming, consuming both their financial resources and emotional energy. During one particularly tense meeting with their lawyers, Aadir addressed his team. "We're going to fight this. We've worked too hard to let baseless accusations destroy us. Stay focused and trust our process." The legal proceedings dragged on for months, but the ordeal united the team in their resolve. They pored over technical documents, patent filings, and prior art, building a solid defense. Finally, the day of the court ruling arrived. Aadir, Paravi, and Vadish sat in the courtroom, their nerves on edge. The judge reviewed the evidence and delivered the verdict: the competitor's claims were dismissed. The victory was a huge relief. As they left the courtroom, their lawyer turned to them with a smile. "You did it. This is a big win for EcoInnovate."

Back at their office, the atmosphere was celebratory. The team gathered for an impromptu meeting, and Aadir stood before them, filled with gratitude. "We've faced some tough challenges recently," he began, "but we've come through stronger. This legal battle was a harsh reminder of the realities of the business world, but it's also shown me the incredible resilience of our team." Paravi nodded. "We can't let setbacks define us. We've proven we can overcome anything." Vadish added, "And we've learned valuable lessons along the way. We need to stay vigilant and continue innovating." Aadir smiled, feeling a renewed sense of purpose. "Let's keep pushing forward. This is just the beginning of what we can achieve together." The setbacks had tested their resilience and unity, but they had emerged victorious. As they celebrated their victory, Aadir knew that the future held even greater challenges and opportunities. But with his team by his side, he was ready to face them head-on.

After weathering the storm of setbacks, EcoInnovate was on the cusp of a major breakthrough. Aadir and his team had poured their hearts and souls into developing a new product that had the potential to revolutionize the energy industry. The excitement in the air was palpable as they prepared for the final stages of testing and the much-anticipated market launch.

In the lab, Vadish held the prototype in his hands, a glint of excitement in his eyes. "This could be it, Aadir. Our breakthrough." Aadir nodded, a surge of anticipation coursing through him. "Let's run the final tests. If everything checks out, we're ready for the market." The testing process was rigorous, with every aspect of the device scrutinized and evaluated. As the results came in, the team's confidence soared. The new energy storage device exceeded their expectations, boasting unparalleled efficiency and reliability. "This is it," Paravi exclaimed, studying the test data. "We've done it."

The day of the market launch arrived, and EcoInnovate spared no expense in ensuring it was a grand affair. The venue was adorned with banners and displays showcasing their latest innovation, and industry leaders, investors, and media representatives filled the room with anticipation. Aadir took the stage, his heart pounding with excitement and nerves. "Ladies and gentlemen, thank you for joining us today. It gives me immense pleasure to introduce EcoInnovate's latest breakthrough in energy storage technology." As he unveiled the product, the room erupted in applause. Aadir's presentation highlighted the device's groundbreaking features and its potential to transform the energy landscape.

The response was overwhelmingly positive. Orders flooded in from eager customers, and the media coverage was glowing. EcoInnovate's new product was hailed as a game-changer, a testament to their relentless pursuit of innovation and excellence. As Aadir fielded questions from reporters and investors, he felt a sense of pride and satisfaction. This was more than just a product launch; it was a validation of everything they had worked for. In the weeks that followed, EcoInnovate's success brought a flood of opportunities. They received partnership offers from major corporations, invitations to collaborate on international projects, and interest from government agencies seeking to adopt their technology for sustainable development initiatives.

Aadir reflected on the journey they had taken, from humble beginnings to becoming a recognized leader in the field of renewable energy. The road had been fraught with challenges and setbacks, but their unwavering determination had propelled them forward. As he stood at the helm of EcoInnovate, Aadir knew somewhere that their journey was far from over. But with their breakthrough success behind them, they were ready to face whatever challenges lay ahead, armed with innovation, resilience, and a shared vision for a sustainable future.

TWELVE

As EcoInnovate soared to new heights of success, Aadir's thoughts turned to the community that had shaped him. He felt a deep-rooted desire to give back, to create opportunities for those who, like him, had once faced seemingly insurmountable obstacles. With this in mind, he embarked on a mission to establish initiatives aimed at empowering the underprivileged and fostering a culture of innovation and education.

The EcoInnovate Foundation was born, a beacon of hope for those in need. Its primary focus was on promoting education and innovation in rural areas, where resources were scarce and opportunities limited. Aadir poured his heart and soul into this endeavor, determined to make a tangible difference in the lives of others. The foundation's first initiative was to fund scholarships for underprivileged students, providing them with access to quality education and the opportunity to pursue their dreams. Aadir believed firmly in the transformative power of education and was determined to ensure that no deserving student was held back by financial constraints.

In addition to scholarships, the foundation set out to improve educational infrastructure in rural schools. Aadir remembered his own humble beginnings and the lack of resources he had faced. He was determined to change that for future generations. Thus, the foundation embarked on a mission to equip schools with modern facilities, starting with Aadir's own alma mater in Kashi. The inauguration of the newly equipped science lab was a momentous occasion, filled with hope and promise. Aadir addressed the students, his voice filled with passion and determination. "This lab is not just a room filled with equipment. It's a gateway to endless possibilities, a place where your dreams can take flight. Explore, experiment, and never stop dreaming."

As the foundation's initiatives gained momentum, Aadir realized the importance of mentorship in nurturing young talent. Thus, the foundation launched a mentorship program, connecting students with professionals in various fields. Aadir himself took on several mentees, guiding them through their academic and personal journeys with compassion and wisdom. Paravi, who spearheaded the foundation's operations, played a crucial role in its success. "We're not just providing resources," she explained. "We're creating a support system, nurturing talent, and building a community of innovators who will shape the future."

The impact of the foundation was profound and far-reaching. Students who had once felt trapped by their circumstances now dared to dream of a brighter future. Aspiring engineers, scientists, and entrepreneurs emerged from the most unlikely of places, fueled by the belief that anything was possible. Aadir felt a profound sense of fulfillment, knowing that he was making a tangible difference in the lives of others. With each scholarship awarded, each science lab inaugurated, and each mentee guided, he knew that he was leaving behind a legacy of hope, empowerment, and possibility. And for Aadir, that was the greatest achievement of all.

With EcoInnovate firmly established as a leader in sustainable energy solutions in India, Aadir's vision expanded beyond national borders. He saw immense potential in taking their innovative products and solutions to the global stage. Thus, the journey of international expansion began, marked by challenges, opportunities, and transformative impact.

The decision to expand internationally was not taken lightly. Aadir and his team understood the complexities and risks involved in venturing into new markets. Yet, they were driven by a shared determination to make a global impact and bring their vision of a sustainable future to people around the world. Their first foray into international markets focused on neighboring countries, where they could leverage their knowledge of the region and existing networks. The reception was positive, encouraging them to set their sights on Europe and North America, where the demand for renewable energy solutions was high.

However, expanding internationally presented a myriad of challenges. Regulatory hurdles varied from country to country, cultural differences had to be navigated, and competition was fierce. Aadir and Paravi, undeterred by these obstacles, embarked on a series of fact-finding missions, traveling across continents to explore opportunities and forge partnerships. In China, they encountered complex regulatory frameworks but found a burgeoning market hungry for innovative energy solutions. In Europe, they faced stiff competition from established players but differentiated themselves with their cutting-edge technology. In North America, strategic partnerships with tech giants opened doors to vast opportunities in the burgeoning smart grid sector.

Adaptability became the cornerstone of their international strategy. They hired local experts, conducted exhaustive market research, and customized their products to suit regional needs. Aadir's leadership and strategic vision guided them through the maze of international business, ensuring that they stayed true to their core values while seizing new opportunities. One of the most gratifying experiences of their international expansion journey was setting up an office in Kenya. Partnering with local communities, they brought sustainable energy solutions to rural areas, transforming lives and powering progress in previously underserved regions.

As EcoInnovate expanded its footprint globally, Aadir's role evolved. He delegated more responsibilities to his capable team, empowering them to drive the company's growth while upholding its values and standards. The international expansion was a testament to their collective effort and unwavering commitment to making a positive impact on the world. Reflecting on their journey, Aadir felt a deep sense of pride and gratitude. From humble beginnings in Mumbai to a global leader in renewable energy, EcoInnovate's success was a testament to the power of innovation, resilience, and a shared vision for a better, more sustainable future. And as they looked ahead to the next chapter, Aadir felt excited for the endless possibilities that lay on the horizon.

THIRTEEN

Aadir gets invited to speak at a prestigious global summit on sustainable energy.The invitation was a defining moment for Aadir and EcoInnovate. It was not just an acknowledgment of their achievements but also an opportunity to share their vision with the world and inspire others to join the movement towards a sustainable future.

Preparation for the summit consumed Aadir's days and nights as he meticulously crafted his speech. Drawing from his personal journey and the collective experience of EcoInnovate, he sought to deliver a message that would resonate with the global audience. Paravi and Vadish provided invaluable feedback, refining his words to ensure maximum impact. As the day of the summit arrived, Aadir felt a surge of anticipation and nerves. Stepping into the grand conference hall, he was greeted by the sight of distinguished guests from around the world. The weight of the moment settled on his shoulders, but he drew strength from the knowledge that he was representing not just himself but a movement fueled by passion and purpose.

Taking the stage, Aadir felt a rush of adrenaline as he began his speech. His voice echoed through the hall, carrying the story of EcoInnovate's journey – the struggles, the triumphs, and the unwavering commitment to sustainability. He spoke of the challenges faced by the world and the urgent need for innovative solutions. "Ladies and gentlemen," he proclaimed, "we stand at a critical juncture in history. The choices we make today will shape the world of tomorrow. EcoInnovate is proof that change is possible, that with determination and ingenuity, we can overcome even the most daunting challenges." His words resonated with the audience, drawing them into his vision of a future powered by renewable energy and sustainable practices. The applause that followed was thunderous, a testament to the impact of his message.

After his speech, Aadir was approached by leaders and experts from various fields, eager to learn from his experience and explore potential collaborations. He found himself engaged in conversations that went beyond business – discussions about the future of the planet, the role of technology in driving change, and the importance of collective action. As the summit drew to a close, Aadir took a moment to soak in the magnitude of the moment. From being a young dreamer with a vision to standing on a global stage, his journey had been nothing short of remarkable. But he knew that this was just the beginning – a stepping stone towards an even greater impact.

As he left the summit, Aadir carried with him a renewed sense of purpose and determination. The experience had reaffirmed his belief in the power of individuals to effect change and the importance of coming together as a global community to tackle the challenges that lay ahead. With EcoInnovate by his side, he was ready to continue leading the charge towards a more sustainable future, one innovation at a time.

FOURTEEN

With EcoInnovate's global expansion well underway, Aadir wanted to ensure that innovation remained at the heart of their mission. He proposed the creation of an innovation lab, a dedicated space for the research and development of cutting-edge sustainable technologies. This would be a place where ideas could flourish, where scientists, engineers, and visionaries from around the world could collaborate to create a more sustainable future.

At the quarterly board meeting, Aadir presented his vision. "We've accomplished so much in our journey to expand globally," Aadir began, his eyes shining with excitement. "But we must ensure that innovation remains our core focus. I propose the creation of an innovation lab, a dedicated space for research and development, where the brightest minds can come together to develop the sustainable technologies of tomorrow." The board members exchanged intrigued glances. "Tell us more," said Meera, the head of operations. "How do you envision this lab functioning?"

Aadir outlined his plan. The lab would be designed as a collaborative environment, equipped with state-of-the-art facilities and resources. He would recruit top talent from around the world, fostering an open culture where ideas could be freely shared and explored. "It's not just about the technology," Aadir explained. "It's about creating an ecosystem of innovation, where creativity and collaboration drive meaningful change." The board unanimously approved the proposal. Within months, the innovation lab was established, a sleek, modern building filled with cutting-edge equipment and a diverse team of experts.

One of the lab's first projects was developing a new type of solar panel that used advanced materials to increase efficiency and reduce costs. The team, led by Vadish, a renowned materials scientist, worked tirelessly, experimenting with different materials and configurations. One afternoon, after months of research and testing, Vadish called for a team meeting. The room buzzed with anticipation as he revealed their findings. "This new panel can generate 20% more energy than current models," Vadish announced, holding up a prototype. "It's a significant improvement and could revolutionize the solar industry." Aadir, who was present at the meeting, couldn't hide his excitement. "This is exactly why we created the innovation lab," he said, his voice filled with pride. "Let's prepare for production and start rolling these out."

Another exciting project was the development of a smart grid system that used artificial intelligence to optimize energy distribution. The system could predict energy demand, manage supply in real-time, and reduce waste. The lab collaborated with universities and tech companies to refine the technology. During a brainstorming session, the team discussed the potential impact of the smart grid. "If we can accurately predict energy demand and optimize distribution," explained Lila, a data scientist on the team, "we can significantly reduce waste and improve efficiency. It's a game-changer for sustainable energy." Aadir nodded in agreement. "And by partnering with universities and tech companies, we're ensuring that this technology is at the forefront of innovation. This is exactly the kind of collaboration we need."

The innovation lab also focused on education and community engagement. They hosted workshops and hackathons, inviting students and young professionals to contribute their ideas and solutions. Aadir personally mentored many of the participants, fostering a new generation of innovators. One day, Aadir found himself talking to a group of students at a workshop. "Innovation isn't just about having the best technology," he said. "It's about thinking differently, challenging the status quo, and believing that you can make a difference."

The lab's success underscored EcoInnovate's commitment to continuous improvement and innovation. Aadir felt proud of the collaborative spirit and the groundbreaking work being done. The innovation lab was not just about technology; it was about inspiring creativity and driving meaningful change. At the annual company meeting, Aadir took a moment to reflect on the journey. "We've made incredible strides this year," he said. "The work being done at the innovation lab is a testament to what we can achieve when we come together with a shared vision. It's not just about creating sustainable technologies; it's about building a better future for everyone." The room erupted in applause, a celebration of their collective achievements and a reaffirmation of their commitment to innovation. Aadir knew that this was just the beginning. With the innovation lab leading the way, the future looked brighter than ever.

FIFTEEN

Amid the professional successes, Aadir's personal life also saw significant milestones. One of the most profound moments was reconciling with his estranged mother. After years of distance, Aadir reached out, wanting to bridge the gap that had formed between them.

One evening, as Aadir sat alone in his apartment in Mumbai, he stared at the phone. He had been contemplating this call for weeks. Taking a deep breath, he dialed his mother's number. "Hello?" Her voice was cautious but familiar. "Hi, Mom. It's Aadir," he said, his voice trembling slightly. "I... I was hoping we could talk." There was a moment of silence before she responded. "I'd like that, Aadir. I've missed you." Aadir invited his mother to Mumbai.

When she arrived, they spent time talking and reconnecting. They sat in a quiet café, the aroma of coffee mingling with the hum of conversation around them. "I've wanted to reach out for so long," Aadir began. "I've been through a lot, and I want to share my journey with you." His mother nodded, tears welling in her eyes. "I'm proud of you, Aadir. I've followed your success from a distance, and it's incredible what you've achieved. I'm sorry I wasn't there for you when you needed me." Aadir felt a weight lift off his shoulders. "We can't change the past, but we can move forward. I want us to be part of each other's lives." They talked for hours, sharing stories and bridging the years of separation.

The reconciliation brought a sense of peace and closure. Aadir's mother began visiting more often, becoming a part of his support system. The renewed relationship enriched his life, providing a personal anchor amid the professional whirlwind.

It was the last day of the sustainability conference, and Aadir was exhausted but exhilarated. He had just finished giving a talk when a young woman approached him. "That was an inspiring speech, Aadir," she said, smiling. "I'm Snigdha." Aadir shook her hand, intrigued. "Thank you, Snigdha. What brings you to the conference?" "I'm an environmentalist, working on community-led conservation projects. Your work with EcoInnovate aligns so much with what I believe in." Their conversation flowed naturally, and Aadir found himself drawn to her passion and vision. Over the next few weeks, they met frequently, discussing ideas and sharing experiences. One evening, as they walked along the beach, Snigdha turned to Aadir. "You know, I've always felt a strong connection with you. It's more than just our shared work." Aadir stopped, looking into her eyes. "I feel the same way, Snigdha. You've brought so much joy and balance into my life." Their relationship blossomed, and Snigdha became a cherished part of Aadir's life. She supported his work, offered valuable insights, and helped him navigate the pressures of leadership. Together, they envisioned new projects and initiatives, blending their personal and professional lives. These personal milestones influenced Aadir's leadership. He became more empathetic and focused on fostering a supportive and inclusive culture within EcoInnovate. He encouraged his team to prioritize their well-being and maintain a healthy work-life balance.

SIXTEEN

It was the last day of the sustainability conference, and Aadir was exhausted but exhilarated. He had just finished giving a talk when a young woman approached him. "That was an inspiring speech, Aadir," she said, smiling. "I'm Snigdha." Aadir shook her hand, intrigued. "Thank you, Snigdha. What brings you to the conference?" "I'm an environmentalist, working on community-led conservation projects. Your work with EcoInnovate aligns so much with what I believe in." Their conversation flowed naturally, and Aadir found himself drawn to her passion and vision.

Over the next few weeks, they met frequently, discussing ideas and sharing experiences. One evening, as they walked along the beach, Snigdha turned to Aadir. "You know, I've always felt a strong connection with you. It's more than just our shared work." Aadir stopped, looking into her eyes. "I feel the same way, Snigdha. You've brought so much joy and balance into my life."

Their relationship blossomed, and Snigdha became a cherished part of Aadir's life. She supported his work, offered valuable insights, and helped him navigate the pressures of leadership. Together, they envisioned new projects and initiatives, blending their personal and professional lives. These personal milestones influenced Aadir's leadership. He became more empathetic and focused on fostering a supportive and inclusive culture within EcoInnovate. He encouraged his team to prioritize their well-being and maintain a healthy work-life balance.

SEVENTEEN

EcoInnovate's commitment to sustainability extended beyond individual products and technologies. Aadir envisioned creating entire communities that embodied sustainable living. He partnered with governments and organizations to develop model sustainable communities, beginning with a flagship project in Maharashtra.

At a high-level meeting with government officials and potential partners, Aadir outlined his ambitious plan. "Imagine a village where every home is powered by renewable energy, where water is conserved and reused, and where organic farming supports local food needs," Aadir said, his passion evident. "This is not just an eco-friendly initiative; it's a model for sustainable living." The officials were intrigued. "This could be transformative for rural development," said Rajesh, the state's minister for rural affairs. "But we must ensure the local community is fully engaged in this process." Aadir agreed. "Community involvement is crucial. We need to work with the residents to understand their needs and ensure they feel a sense of ownership over the project."

EcoInnovate's team spent months planning and implementing the project. They collaborated closely with local authorities and involved the residents at every stage. Meetings were held in the village community hall, where Aadir and his team listened to the villagers' concerns and ideas. During one of these meetings, Aadir stood before a room filled with curious and hopeful faces. "We're here to build something together. Your input is vital to making this community truly sustainable and tailored to your needs." An elderly farmer, Ramesh, raised his hand. "We need better irrigation systems. Can we use the rainwater harvesting for our crops?" Aadir smiled. "Absolutely, Ramesh. Rainwater harvesting will be a key component of this project. We'll ensure it supports both household and agricultural needs."

The team worked tirelessly, designing solar-powered homes, installing rainwater harvesting systems, and setting up organic farming plots. They also constructed educational facilities, healthcare centers, and recreational spaces, all designed with sustainability in mind.

The project's completion was marked by an inauguration ceremony attended by local residents, government officials, and EcoInnovate team members. The atmosphere was celebratory as villagers gathered to see their new community officially launched. Standing before the crowd, Aadir addressed the villagers. "This project is not just about buildings and technology. It's about creating a way of life that respects and nurtures our environment. Together, we're building a sustainable future." The villagers applauded, their faces glowing with pride and excitement. The sense of community was palpable.

The impact of the project was profound. The village became a model for sustainable living, attracting visitors and researchers from around the world. It demonstrated the feasibility and benefits of integrated sustainability, inspiring similar projects in other regions. A few months later, Aadir met with a delegation from another state interested in replicating the project. "Your work in Maharashtra has shown us what's possible," said Anjali, the delegation leader. "We'd like to explore how we can implement similar initiatives in our region." Aadir nodded, feeling a deep sense of accomplishment. "We're eager to help. Sustainable communities are the future, and we're committed to spreading this model wherever it's needed."

EcoInnovate also collaborated with urban planners to retrofit existing neighborhoods with green infrastructure. In Mumbai, they worked on converting a densely populated area into a sustainable urban oasis. The project included green roofs, energy-efficient buildings, and community gardens. During a site visit, Aadir met with the urban planning team. "This area has so much potential," he said, looking out over the cityscape. "By integrating green infrastructure, we can drastically reduce the environmental footprint and improve quality of life for residents." The urban planner, Arjun, explained their approach. "We're focusing on retrofitting existing buildings with energy-efficient technologies and creating green spaces that serve as community hubs. The goal is to make sustainability accessible and beneficial for everyone."

The success of these projects reinforced EcoInnovate's reputation as a leader in sustainable development. Media coverage and public interest soared, and Aadir found himself speaking at international conferences about the potential of sustainable communities. At one such conference, a reporter asked, "What drives you to pursue these large-scale sustainable projects?" Aadir paused, reflecting on his journey. "It's about creating a legacy of positive change. By building sustainable communities, we're not only addressing environmental challenges but also enhancing the quality of life for people. It's a holistic approach to development that I believe can transform our world."

Aadir's vision of creating sustainable communities had become a reality. The projects in Maharashtra and Mumbai showcased the potential of innovative solutions to transform lives and environments. As EcoInnovate continued to grow, Aadir remained committed to pushing the boundaries of what was possible, driven by the belief that sustainability and community well-being were inextricably linked.

EIGHTEEN

Despite their successes, EcoInnovate faced new challenges. An economic downturn led to reduced funding and increased competition in the technology sector. Aadir and his team had to navigate these obstacles while maintaining their commitment to innovation and sustainability.

The first signs of trouble came with a sudden drop in funding. Investors were cautious, and budgets were tight. Aadir called an emergency meeting with his senior team to discuss the financial situation. "We're facing a significant reduction in funding," Aadir said, his tone serious but calm. "We need to prioritize projects and optimize our resources to navigate this period." Meera, the head of operations, suggested, "We should arrange a meeting with the investors." Aadir nodded. "Indeed Meera , we will do so once all the investors are available".

In the following weeks, the team held several brainstorming sessions. They assessed each project's impact and viability, deciding which to pursue and which to put on hold. During one such session, Ravi, the lead engineer, raised a concern. "We've been working on the new smart grid system for months. It's crucial, but it's also expensive. Should we continue?" Aadir considered this. "The smart grid system has immense potential for long-term impact. Let's find ways to streamline the process and cut unnecessary costs. We can't afford to abandon it, but we need to be smarter about how we proceed." Meanwhile, the day of meeting with investors arrived.

The conference room at EcoInnovate was unusually tense. Aadir and Snigdha,his partner and a passionate environmentalist, sat across from a group of investors, their expressions serious. "We appreciate your interest in our work," one investor said, adjusting his glasses. "But the recent political changes in the region are causing us to reconsider our commitment. The risk factors have increased significantly." Aadir leaned forward, his tone measured. "We understand the concerns, but the need for sustainable solutions hasn't diminished. If anything, it's more critical now." Snigdha added, "Our projects have already shown significant impact. With your continued support, we can navigate these challenges and ensure long-term success." The investors exchanged glances, their skepticism clear. "We'll need to see a revised risk assessment and contingency plans before we can move forward," another investor said.

As the meeting concluded, Aadir and Snigdha walked back to their office in silence. The weight of the situation pressed heavily on their shoulders. "This isn't what we expected," Snigdha said finally, breaking the silence. "We need that funding to keep our projects alive." Aadir nodded, frustration evident in his voice. "We'll figure it out. Let's regroup and strategize. We can't let this stop us." They gathered the team for an emergency meeting. Aadir outlined the situation, and the room fell silent. "We need solutions," he said, looking around the table. "How do we secure the funding and navigate the political landscape?" One team member suggested diversifying their funding sources. "We can approach foundations and NGOs that focus on sustainable development. They might be more flexible and mission-aligned." Snigdha agreed. "We should also look into crowdfunding. It's risky, but it could generate enough interest and support from the public." As they brainstormed, new ideas emerged. They decided to host a high-profile event to showcase their successes and attract potential donors and partners. They also planned to reach out to media outlets to raise awareness about their work and the challenges they faced. The following weeks were a whirlwind of activity.

Snigdha and Aadir worked tirelessly, meeting with potential partners, revising proposals, and preparing for the event. Their dedication inspired the team, but the stress took its toll. One evening, after a particularly grueling day, Snigdha found Aadir in his office, staring at his computer screen. She knocked softly on the door. "Hey," she said, her voice gentle. "You okay?" Aadir looked up, exhaustion etched on his face. "Just trying to figure out our next move. It's overwhelming." Snigdha sat down across from him. "We'll get through this. We've faced challenges before, and we've come out stronger." Aadir sighed, running a hand through his hair. "I know. It's just... sometimes it feels like we're fighting a losing battle." Snigdha reached out, placing her hand on his. "We're in this together. We'll find a way." Their words of encouragement fueled their resolve. They doubled down on their efforts, rallying the team and pushing through the obstacles. The event was a success, drawing attention and support from unexpected quarters. New partnerships formed, and alternative funding came through. Slowly but surely, they stabilized their projects and regained momentum. As they looked back on the turbulent months, Aadir and Snigdha realized that their setbacks had only strengthened their bond and commitment. They had proven that even in the face of adversity, their vision and determination could overcome any challenge.

At the same time, technological competition intensified. New startups and established companies entered the sustainable energy market, challenging EcoInnovate's market position. Aadir called another meeting to address this issue. "We're facing stiff competition," Aadir began. "Our strength has always been our innovation and our commitment to our customers. We need to double down on both." Lila, a data scientist, suggested, "We should increase our investment in research and development. Explore new technologies and improve our existing products." "And we need to strengthen our relationships with customers," added Snigdha. "Gather their feedback and incorporate it into our designs. Make sure they know we're listening and responding to their needs."

The team took these suggestions to heart. They ramped up their R&D efforts, working on cutting-edge technologies and refining their existing products. They also launched a series of customer engagement initiatives, including surveys, focus groups, and interactive webinars. One of their significant triumphs was the development of a new energy-efficient cooling system. During a demonstration at the lab, Vadish, the materials scientist, showcased the system's capabilities. "This new cooling system uses advanced materials that significantly reduce energy consumption," Vadish explained. "It's a game-changer for both residential and commercial use." The product received widespread acclaim, helping EcoInnovate regain its competitive edge. During a team celebration, Aadir took a moment to acknowledge everyone's efforts. "This success is a testament to our resilience and our commitment to innovation," he said, raising a glass. "We've faced challenges head-on and emerged stronger. I'm incredibly proud of what we've accomplished together."

The experiences taught Aadir valuable lessons in adaptability and strategic thinking. He became more attuned to market trends and proactive in identifying opportunities and threats. During a leadership retreat, he shared his reflections with his team. "We've learned the importance of staying flexible and being proactive," Aadir said. "We've faced economic challenges and fierce competition, but we've adapted and thrived. It's made us stronger as a team and as a company." The challenges also strengthened the team's unity and resolve. They developed a deeper sense of trust and collaboration, knowing they could rely on each other in difficult times.

As Ecoinnovate continued to grow, Aadir remained committed to pushing the boundaries of what was possible. He knew that the road ahead would have its challenges, but he also knew that his team was capable of overcoming any obstacle. In a closing meeting with his leadership team, Aadir reiterated his vision. "Our mission is to drive sustainable innovation. We've proven that we can navigate tough times and come out stronger. Let's continue to lead with passion and purpose, knowing that we're making a real difference in the world." With renewed determination, EcoInnovate moved forward, ready to face whatever challenges lay ahead. Aadir and his team had learned that with resilience, adaptability, and a strong sense of mission, they could overcome any hurdle and continue to innovate for a sustainable future.

NINETEEN

The sun was setting as Aadir and Snigdha walked through the fields, the sky painted in hues of orange and pink. Their days were filled with work, but the evenings were their time to unwind and talk.

"You know, Aadir," Snigdha said, breaking the comfortable silence, "I've always admired your vision and determination. You've inspired so many people, including me."

Aadir looked at her, his expression softening. "I couldn't have done it without you. You've been my rock through all this. Your passion and dedication are contagious." They paused at a clearing, the cool breeze rustling the leaves. Snigdha turned to Aadir, her eyes reflecting the setting sun. "Aadir, I have to admit something. Over these past few months, I've grown to care about you deeply. More than just a friend." Aadir's heart skipped a beat. He had felt the same but was unsure how to express it. "Snigdha, I feel the same way. You've been more than a friend to me. You've been my partner, my confidant, and now... I hope, my love." Snigdha smiled, tears glistening in her eyes. "Yes, Aadir. I want to share this journey with you, both professionally and personally."

Aadir reached out, taking her hand in his. "Together, we can achieve anything." Their relationship deepened, and their love for each other grew stronger with each passing day. They supported each other through challenges, celebrated successes, and found joy in the simple moments of life.

TWENTY

Meanwhile,EcoInnovate's perseverance and innovation paid off, solidifying their position as a global leader in sustainable technology. Their products and solutions were used in over 50 countries, impacting millions of lives and environments. The journey was long and filled with challenges, but Aadir and his team had remained steadfast in their mission.

EcoInnovate's achievements were recognized globally. Aadir received numerous accolades for his leadership and contributions to sustainability. He was invited to speak at prestigious conferences and events, where he shared EcoInnovate's journey and vision for a sustainable future. At the World Economic Forum, Aadir addressed a packed audience. "EcoInnovate started with a simple idea: to harness technology for a sustainable future. Today, our innovations are making a real difference around the world. This is a testament to what we can achieve when we prioritize our planet and our communities." The recognition reinforced EcoInnovate's impact and inspired others to follow their lead. Media coverage highlighted their pioneering projects, from eco-friendly villages in rural India to urban green initiatives in major cities. Aadir's leadership was praised in numerous articles and reports, solidifying his status as a visionary in the field of sustainability.

Reflecting on their journey, Aadir felt a deep sense of pride and gratitude. In an interview with a leading environmental magazine, he shared his thoughts. "We've come a long way from being the odd one out," Aadir said, smiling. "In the early days, our ideas seemed unconventional and impractical to many. But we persevered because we believed in our mission. Today, seeing the impact we've made, I know it was all worth it." The interviewer asked, "What's next for EcoInnovate?" Aadir's eyes sparkled with enthusiasm. "Our journey is far from over. We have a responsibility to continue pushing the boundaries of innovation and sustainability. There are still many challenges to tackle, from climate change to social equity. We're expanding our mission to address these broader societal goals."

Looking to the future, Aadir envisioned new projects and initiatives. He gathered his leadership team to discuss the next steps. "We have the technology and the talent to create a better world," Aadir said during the meeting. "But it requires collaboration, determination, and a shared commitment to making a difference. Together, we can build a future that is sustainable, equitable, and prosperous for all." Meera, the head of operations, proposed a new initiative focused on renewable energy access in developing countries. "Many regions still lack reliable energy sources. We could develop affordable solar and wind solutions tailored to these areas." "That's a great idea, Meera," Aadir replied. "Energy access is fundamental to development. Let's prioritize this project." Snigdha, Aadir's partner and a passionate environmentalist, suggested expanding their educational programs. "We should invest in educating the next generation about sustainability. Our workshops and hackathons have been successful; let's scale them up globally." Aadir agreed. "Education is key to long-term change. Let's partner with schools and universities to make this happen."

Aadir remained at the helm, guiding the company with his vision and values. He knew that the journey ahead would be filled with challenges and uncertainties, but he was confident in their ability to overcome them. During a company-wide meeting, Aadir addressed all employees, both in-person and remotely. "We've achieved so much together, but our work is not done. We must remain committed to our mission and be ready to face new challenges head-on. Our goal is not just to lead in technology but to lead in creating a sustainable and equitable world." The employees cheered, inspired by Aadir's words. There was a palpable sense of unity and purpose within the company.

With a renewed sense of purpose and determination, Aadir and his team embarked on the next chapter of EcoInnovate's journey. They launched new projects aimed at addressing global challenges, from renewable energy initiatives in underserved regions to large-scale urban sustainability programs. EcoInnovate also expanded its partnerships, working with international organizations, governments, and other companies to amplify their impact. They continued to innovate, developing new technologies that pushed the boundaries of what was possible in sustainability. Aadir remained a visible and active leader, continuously engaging with stakeholders and sharing EcoInnovate's vision. At a global sustainability summit, he concluded his keynote speech with a powerful message. "The future is ours to shape. By working together, leveraging our strengths, and staying committed to our values, we can create a world that is not only sustainable but also just and prosperous. This is our legacy, and I am confident that we will continue to drive change for generations to come." As the audience erupted in applause, Aadir felt a deep sense of fulfillment. EcoInnovate's journey was far from over, and with his dedicated team by his side, he looked forward to the challenges and opportunities that lay ahead. Together, they were not just creating a company—they were building a movement for a better world.

As news of the unfolding environmental crisis spread, Aadir called for an emergency meeting with his team at EcoInnovate. The atmosphere in the conference room was tense, filled with a sense of urgency and determination.

"We can't sit idly by while the world faces this crisis," Aadir said, his voice resolute as he looked around the room. "We need to mobilize our resources and expertise to develop innovative solutions that can make a real difference." Vadish, EcoInnovate's lead engineer, nodded in agreement. "We have the technology and the talent to tackle this challenge head-on. Let's brainstorm ideas and come up with a plan of action." The team, consisting of engineers, scientists, and sustainability experts, began brainstorming immediately. Flip charts filled with ideas and concepts quickly filled the room. "We need to address carbon emissions first," suggested Meera, head of operations. "Reducing and sequestering CO2 should be our top priority." Paravi, EcoInnovate's chief scientist, spoke up. "I've been working on bio-based materials that can absorb and store carbon dioxide from the atmosphere. These materials have the potential to capture large amounts of CO2 and convert it into a stable form." Aadir was intrigued. "How can we deploy these materials quickly and effectively?"

Paravi explained the concept further. "We can integrate these materials into construction projects, agriculture, and even produce carbon-negative fuels. For instance, in construction, these materials can replace traditional concrete, absorbing CO2 as they cure and over their lifespan." The room buzzed with excitement. Aadir saw the potential. "This could be a game-changer in our fight against climate change. Let's fast-track the development and deployment of these materials." Vadish suggested another approach. "We could also develop enhanced natural systems for carbon capture. Planting genetically optimized trees and algae that can absorb CO2 at higher rates." Snigdha, who was also present, added, "And we mustn't forget community resilience. We should work on technologies that help communities adapt to the changing climate, like advanced irrigation systems for drought-prone areas and flood barriers for regions at risk of rising sea levels." Aadir agreed. "Let's form dedicated teams for each of these initiatives. We need to work simultaneously on multiple fronts to address this crisis comprehensively."

The team divided into groups, each focusing on a specific solution. They worked around the clock, collaborating with external researchers, universities, and other tech companies. Aadir personally reached out to international organizations, securing partnerships and funding to support their initiatives. One of their significant collaborations was with a leading university in Europe known for its cutting-edge environmental research. Together, they accelerated the development of the bio-based materials. Paravi traveled to the university's labs to oversee the joint research. "We need to test these materials in various conditions to ensure their effectiveness," she explained to the university's lead scientist. "The faster we can confirm their stability and carbon absorption rates, the sooner we can deploy them." Meanwhile, Meera's team focused on the genetically optimized trees and algae. They set up test sites in different climatic zones to monitor growth rates and CO2 absorption. "These natural systems could be a vital part of our carbon capture strategy," Meera said during a site visit. "It's essential we get this right."

Despite the challenges, EcoInnovate's efforts paid off. Within months, they began deploying the bio-based materials in construction projects across the globe. The initial results were promising, with buildings constructed using these materials showing significant CO2 absorption. During a project launch in Brazil, Aadir stood beside the local mayor. "This building represents the future of sustainable construction," he said. "It's not just about reducing emissions; it's about reversing the damage we've already done." In parallel, the genetically optimized trees and algae showed remarkable growth and CO2 absorption rates. Meera's team expanded the test sites into large-scale plantations, working with local communities to ensure sustainable management. The irrigation and flood barrier systems also saw successful implementations. In a drought-prone region in Africa, Snigdha oversaw the installation of advanced irrigation systems. "These systems will not only conserve water but also increase crop yields, helping the community adapt to the changing climate," she said.

EcoInnovate's innovative solutions played a crucial role in mitigating the environmental crisis. Governments and organizations worldwide recognized their contributions, and Aadir was invited to speak at numerous international forums. At the United Nations Climate Change Conference, Aadir delivered a keynote address. "The crisis we face is unprecedented, but so is our capacity for innovation and collaboration," he said. "EcoInnovate's journey has shown that by working together, we can develop solutions that make a real difference." Reflecting on their journey, Aadir felt a deep sense of pride and gratitude. In an interview with a leading environmental magazine, he shared his thoughts. "We've come a long way, but our journey is far from over. We have a responsibility to continue pushing the boundaries of innovation and sustainability."

TWENTY-ONE

Aadir paced the halls of EcoInnovate's research facility, deep in thought. The company was on the cusp of a technological breakthrough that could revolutionize the renewable energy industry. "We need to push the boundaries of innovation," Aadir said to Vadish, his lead engineer. "We can't afford to be complacent when it comes to developing sustainable technologies." Vadish nodded, his mind already racing with ideas. "I have a few concepts that I've been working on. I think they have the potential to transform the way we harness renewable energy." "Let's hear them," Aadir encouraged, eager to dive into the possibilities. Vadish pulled up a series of schematics on his tablet. "Firstly, we're looking at a new type of solar panel. It uses advanced materials that allow it to generate electricity even in low-light conditions. This would be a game-changer for regions that don't get consistent sunlight." Aadir examined the designs closely. "This could significantly increase solar adoption in areas that previously couldn't rely on solar power. What about wind energy?" "We're developing a vertical-axis wind turbine that's more efficient and less intrusive than traditional models," Vadish explained. "It's designed to operate at lower wind speeds, which makes it viable for urban settings." "Impressive," Aadir said, his excitement growing. "And energy storage?" "We're working on a modular battery system using a new type of electrolyte that improves energy density and cycle life," Vadish replied. "These batteries can store more energy and last longer, making them ideal for integrating with our renewable energy systems."

After weeks of research and experimentation, the team achieved a breakthrough. Vadish gathered everyone in the main lab to unveil their latest innovation—a highly efficient solar panel capable of generating electricity even in low-light conditions. "This could revolutionize the solar energy industry," Paravi exclaimed, her eyes shining with excitement as she inspected the prototype. "Imagine the impact we could have on global energy systems." Aadir smiled, feeling a sense of pride in his team's ingenuity and determination. "This is incredible work, Vadish. Let's get to work on scaling up production and deploying these panels in communities that need them the most."

The team immediately set to work on scaling up the production of their new solar panels. Aadir coordinated with the operations team to streamline the manufacturing process, ensuring they could produce the panels at a competitive cost. "Quality control is paramount," Meera, head of operations, emphasized during a meeting. "We need to ensure these panels perform consistently and reliably in diverse conditions." "We'll set up rigorous testing protocols," Vadish assured her. "We can't afford any setbacks at this stage." Aadir also reached out to potential partners and stakeholders to facilitate the deployment of the new technology. He organized meetings with government officials, NGOs, and private companies to discuss collaboration opportunities. "We believe this technology can make a significant impact," Aadir explained during a meeting with a group of international delegates. "By working together, we can bring sustainable energy to communities worldwide and help reduce our global carbon footprint." The response was overwhelmingly positive. Governments saw the potential to meet their renewable energy targets, NGOs recognized the benefits for underserved communities, and private companies were eager to invest in the groundbreaking technology.

Despite the excitement, the team faced numerous challenges in scaling up implementation. Manufacturing the advanced materials required for the solar panels was complex, and ensuring a stable supply chain was critical. "We need to secure reliable suppliers for the rare materials used in these panels," Vadish reported during a strategy session. "Disruptions in the supply chain could delay our rollout." "I'll handle negotiations with suppliers," Meera said. "We need to establish long-term contracts and diversify our sources to mitigate risks." Logistics also posed a challenge. Distributing the panels to remote and underserved areas required meticulous planning and coordination. "We need to work closely with local partners to ensure smooth delivery and installation," Aadir stated. "Let's leverage our existing networks and build new ones where necessary."

As the production ramped up, EcoInnovate began deploying the new solar panels in targeted regions. The initial projects focused on rural areas with limited access to electricity. In one such village in India, the impact was immediate and profound. Aadir visited the village for the launch ceremony. The community gathered as the first panels were installed on their homes and community buildings. "This is a new beginning for us," said Ramesh, a local resident. "With reliable electricity, we can improve our children's education and support local businesses." Aadir addressed the villagers, feeling a deep sense of fulfillment. "This project is a testament to what we can achieve when we combine innovation with a commitment to sustainability. These panels will provide clean, reliable energy for years to come." The deployment continued across different regions, each project reinforcing the transformative potential of the new technology. As more communities gained access to renewable energy, EcoInnovate's reputation as a global leader in sustainable technology solidified.

With the success of the new solar panels, EcoInnovate continued to push forward. The vertical-axis wind turbines and modular battery systems were next on the agenda, each promising to further enhance the global energy landscape. Aadir reflected on their journey during a team celebration. "We've achieved so much, but there's still a long way to go. Our commitment to innovation and sustainability will guide us as we tackle the next set of challenges." Paravi raised her glass in a toast. "To our team and to the future.

Together, we will continue to drive change and make a lasting impact." The team cheered, energized by their accomplishments and the road ahead. With Aadir's leadership and their collective determination, EcoInnovate was poised to shape the future of renewable energy and sustainability for generations to come.

Aadir met with city officials and urban planners to discuss ways to promote sustainable urban development. They gathered in a conference room overlooking the bustling streets of Mumbai, the cityscape stretching out before them.

"Our cities are facing unprecedented challenges," Aadir said, addressing the group of officials and planners. "But with the right strategies and technologies, we can create urban spaces that are not only livable but also sustainable and resilient." The officials nodded in agreement, eager to explore solutions to the growing problems of congestion, pollution, and resource depletion. Together, they outlined a vision for transforming Mumbai into a model sustainable city. "We need to prioritize green infrastructure and public transportation," Aadir explained. "We also need to invest in renewable energy and energy-efficient buildings to reduce our carbon footprint."

The group brainstormed ideas for green rooftops, urban gardens, and bike-sharing programs, all aimed at promoting sustainable mobility and reducing emissions. "Green rooftops can help mitigate the urban heat island effect and provide insulation for buildings," suggested Priya, an urban planner. "We could incentivize building owners to install them by offering tax breaks or subsidies." "And urban gardens can not only beautify the city but also provide local food sources and reduce our reliance on long-distance transportation," added Raj, a city official. "We could turn underutilized spaces into community gardens." Meera, head of operations at EcoInnovate, chimed in. "We should also look at expanding bike-sharing programs. By creating more bike lanes and making biking safer and more convenient, we can reduce traffic congestion and emissions."

The conversation then turned to renewable energy. They discussed ways to incorporate solar and wind energy into the city's energy systems. "We can install solar panels on rooftops and public buildings," Aadir proposed. "And we should explore the feasibility of wind turbines along the coast. Mumbai has significant potential for both solar and wind energy." Vadish, the lead engineer at EcoInnovate, provided technical insights. "For energy efficiency, we should retrofit existing buildings with advanced insulation and smart energy management systems. New constructions should follow green building standards from the outset."

The group acknowledged the challenges ahead, including funding, public buy-in, and logistical hurdles. "We need to engage the public and educate them on the benefits of these initiatives," suggested Priya. "Public support is crucial for the success of any urban development project." Aadir agreed. "We can launch awareness campaigns and involve community leaders in the planning process. This way, we can ensure that the projects meet the needs and expectations of the residents." Raj highlighted the importance of collaboration. "We need a coordinated effort between the government, private sector, and civil society. EcoInnovate can take the lead on the technology and innovation front, while the government can provide policy support and funding."

With a clear vision and strategy in place, the group began implementing the plan. EcoInnovate partnered with the city to pilot several projects, starting with the installation of solar panels on municipal buildings and the creation of green rooftops in densely populated areas.

Aadir visited one of the first green rooftop projects, a school in central Mumbai. The rooftop was transformed into a lush garden, complete with native plants and vegetable plots. "This garden not only insulates the building but also provides an outdoor classroom for students," Aadir said during a tour with school officials. "It's a living example of how sustainability can be integrated into everyday life."

The city also expanded its public transportation network, adding more electric buses and bike-sharing stations. Meera oversaw the rollout of the bike-sharing program, ensuring that bike lanes were safe and accessible. "By making biking a viable option for short commutes, we're reducing traffic and pollution," Meera explained to a group of reporters. "It's a win-win for the environment and public health."

Meanwhile, Vadish and his team worked on integrating renewable energy sources into the city's power grid. They installed solar panels on rooftops of public buildings and set up small wind turbines along the coast. "We're aiming for a significant portion of the city's energy to come from renewables," Vadish said during a site visit to a newly installed solar array. "This not only reduces emissions but also makes the city more energy-resilient."

To ensure the projects were successful and sustainable, the team set up a monitoring system to track progress and gather feedback from residents. "We're using data analytics to measure the impact of our initiatives," Priya explained. "This helps us make informed decisions and continuously improve our strategies."

Engaging the community was a key part of the plan. EcoInnovate and the city organized workshops and town hall meetings to involve residents in the projects. "By giving people a voice in the process, we're building a sense of ownership and commitment," Aadir said during one such meeting. "Sustainable urban development is about creating spaces that people want to live in and take care of."

The benefits of these initiatives soon became evident. The green rooftops and urban gardens helped cool the city, reduced energy consumption, and provided fresh produce to local communities. The expanded public transportation network reduced traffic congestion and improved air quality. In a follow-up meeting, one of the urban planners remarked, "We have a unique opportunity to lead by example and show the world what's possible. Let's work together to create a city that future generations can be proud of."

Reflecting on the progress, Aadir felt a deep sense of accomplishment. "We've made significant strides, but this is just the beginning," he said to his team. "Our work here in Mumbai can serve as a blueprint for other cities around the world." As EcoInnovate continued to partner with cities and urban planners globally, Aadir remained committed to the vision of sustainable urban development. With each new project, they moved closer to creating a world where cities are not just places to live, but thriving, resilient communities that coexist harmoniously with the environment.

TWENTY-TWO

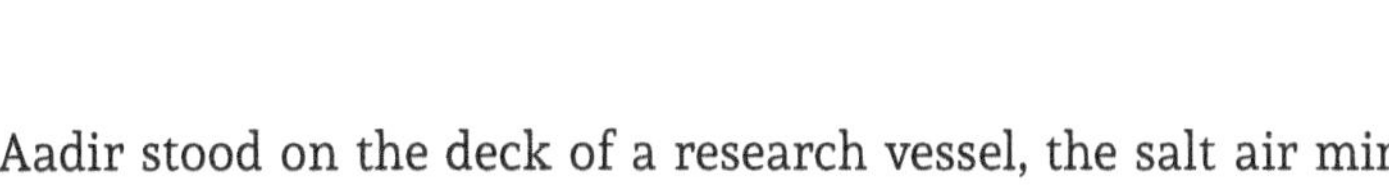

Aadir stood on the deck of a research vessel, the salt air mingling with the sound of crashing waves. He was joined by a team of marine biologists, conservationists, and engineers, all united in their mission to protect the world's oceans. The vessel, named "Ocean Guardian," was equipped with the latest technologies, ready to embark on a crucial mission.

As the team gathered in the ship's conference room, Aadir began the briefing. "The oceans are facing unprecedented threats," he said, addressing the assembled group. "Pollution, overfishing, and habitat destruction are pushing marine ecosystems to the brink. But together, we can make a difference. Let's develop innovative solutions to address these issues head-on." Dr. Sofia Patel, a renowned marine biologist, stepped forward. "Our primary focus will be on tackling plastic pollution, restoring coral reefs, and protecting marine habitats. We have the technology, and now it's time to deploy it effectively."

The team broke into smaller groups, each tasked with brainstorming ideas for specific challenges. In one corner, engineers and biologists discussed potential technologies for cleaning up plastic pollution. "We could develop autonomous drones equipped with sensors and nets to collect plastic waste from the surface of the water," suggested Arun, EcoInnovate's lead engineer. "These drones could patrol the oceans, collecting debris and preventing it from harming marine life." Dr. Patel nodded. "It's a great idea. We should also consider using AI to optimize the drones' routes based on real-time data from satellite imaging."

Back in the lab on the ship, the team set to work. Over the next few weeks, they designed and built prototypes of the autonomous drones. The drones were equipped with advanced sensors to detect plastic waste and nets to collect it. They also included cameras to document their progress and any marine life they encountered. One afternoon, as the team tested a prototype in a large tank, Aadir watched with anticipation. The drone navigated the water, skillfully avoiding obstacles and collecting floating debris. "Impressive," Aadir said, turning to Arun. "How soon can we deploy these drones in the ocean?" Arun smiled. "We're ready for field testing. If all goes well, we can start deploying them in the most affected areas within a month."

The first field test took place near the Great Pacific Garbage Patch. As the drones were deployed into the vast expanse of polluted water, the team monitored their progress from the ship. "Drone Alpha is on course," reported Maya, an engineer, as she watched the live feed. "It's collecting plastic efficiently." Dr. Patel observed the data on her screen. "The drones are also capturing valuable data on water quality and marine life activity. This will help us understand the broader impacts of plastic pollution."

Another critical initiative focused on restoring coral reefs. The team collaborated with local conservationists in the Maldives, an area severely affected by coral bleaching. "We're developing a technique to cultivate and transplant resilient coral species," explained Dr. Patel during a meeting with local partners. "Using underwater nurseries, we can grow corals that are more resistant to temperature changes and then transplant them to affected reefs." Local conservationist Ali Hassan was enthusiastic. "This could significantly boost our reef restoration efforts. Let's combine our expertise and get started."

EcoInnovate also partnered with international organizations to protect marine habitats. They used satellite imaging and underwater drones to map critical habitats and monitor illegal activities such as unregulated fishing. During a strategy session, Aadir emphasized the importance of collaboration. "We need to work with governments, NGOs, and local communities to enforce marine protected areas. Technology can help us monitor these zones, but we need human cooperation to make it effective." *

Recognizing the importance of public engagement, EcoInnovate launched a global campaign to raise awareness about ocean conservation. They created educational materials, organized beach clean-ups, and held workshops in coastal communities. "We need to make ocean conservation a global priority," said Aadir during a press conference. "By educating people about the issues and empowering them to take action, we can create a movement for change."

Despite their efforts, the team faced numerous challenges. Harsh weather conditions, technical failures, and logistical hurdles tested their resilience. Yet, their determination never wavered. During a particularly rough storm, one of the drones malfunctioned. As the team worked tirelessly to repair it, Aadir offered words of encouragement. "Every setback is a learning opportunity. We will fix this and come back stronger."

Gradually, their hard work began to pay off. The autonomous drones collected tons of plastic waste, significantly reducing the pollution in targeted areas. The coral restoration projects showed promising results, with new coral colonies thriving in restored reefs. Marine habitats were better protected, and public awareness grew. One year later, Aadir and his team stood on the same deck of the "Ocean Guardian," looking out at the now cleaner waters. "We've made significant progress," Aadir said, addressing the team. "But our work is far from over. The health of our oceans is crucial for the future of our planet. Let's continue to innovate, collaborate, and fight for a sustainable future." Dr. Patel smiled, reflecting on their journey. "Together, we've shown that it's possible to make a difference. Our oceans still face many challenges, but I'm confident we can overcome them." With renewed determination, the team prepared for the next phase of their mission, ready to continue their fight for ocean conservation and a healthier planet.

TWENTY-THREE

Almost a year and some months went by and the love between Snigdha and Aadir blossomed more beautifully each passing day.Aadir wanted to take the relationship to the next level.

It was a warm evening when Aadir decided to propose to Snigdha. He had chosen a special spot—under the old treehouse where they had spent countless hours together and where their professional collaboration had blossomed into love. Aadir had arranged for a small gathering of friends and family, including his mother, who had become an integral part of his life again. As the sun began to set, casting a golden hue over the horizon, Aadir led Snigdha to the treehouse. "Snigdha, this place holds so many memories for us," Aadir began, his voice filled with emotion. "It's where we dreamed of changing the world, and it's where our love grew." Snigdha looked around, her eyes glistening with tears. "It's perfect, Aadir."

Aadir took a deep breath, then got down on one knee. "Snigdha, you've been my partner, my inspiration, and my love. Will you marry me and continue this journey together, building a future filled with love, hope, and dreams?" Snigdha's eyes filled with tears of joy. "Yes, Aadir! A thousand times, yes!" Their friends and family erupted in cheers, and Aadir slipped the ring onto Snigdha's finger. They embraced, knowing that their future was bright and filled with endless possibilities.

TWENTY-FOUR

Soon after Snigdha said yes, both Aadir and Snigdha resumed work inspite of knowing that their wedding date is finalised on the third day of the next week itself. Aadir's journey to a remote village in rural India marked a pivotal moment for EcoInnovate's mission to combat energy poverty. The sun was setting as he arrived, casting long shadows over the thatched roofs of homes lit by the dim glow of kerosene lamps. The air was tinged with the acrid scent of the burning fuel, a stark reminder of the village's reliance on inefficient and harmful energy sources.

Gathering the villagers under the banyan tree, the traditional meeting spot, Aadir introduced himself and his team from EcoInnovate. The villagers, curious and cautiously hopeful, listened intently as he spoke. "We've come a long way to see how we can help bring change to your community," Aadir began, his voice firm yet warm. "We can't let communities continue to live in darkness and harmful smoke. Together, we can bring clean and affordable energy to every corner of the globe." An elderly man stepped forward, his face weathered from years of living off the land. "We have heard promises before," he said, skepticism laced in his tone. "What makes your promise different?" Aadir nodded, expecting this question. "Our approach is not just to provide temporary solutions, but to empower your community with sustainable energy that you can manage and maintain. We're talking about energy that's clean, renewable, and most importantly, within your control."

With the initial skepticism giving way to a cautious interest, Aadir detailed the plan to deploy off-grid solar energy systems.

"These systems are designed to be simple yet effective. They can power your homes, schools, and health centers without the need for complex infrastructure." The village head, a middle-aged woman named Geeta, expressed her community's needs. "Our children study by lamp light, and our clinic can't store vaccines without reliable refrigeration. This project could change our lives."

Over the next few weeks, EcoInnovate's team, in collaboration with local technicians, began the installation of solar panels across the village. Each household received a small, but powerful solar panel linked to a battery capable of storing energy for nighttime use. Aadir worked alongside the team, teaching the locals how to install and maintain their new systems. "It's important that you know how to take care of these systems," he instructed as they mounted a panel on a roof. "Sustainability is not just about having resources but knowing how to sustain them."

The evening they activated the solar systems was one of celebration. Children watched in awe as electric bulbs lit up their homes for the first time. Their laughter and cheers filled the air, mingling with the sounds of traditional songs played in celebration. A young mother, holding her daughter close, shared her relief with Aadir. "Tonight, for the first time, my children will not breathe in smoke from our lamp. This light is a gift."

The impact of the solar systems extended beyond just lighting homes. The local school could now use computers and educational videos to enhance learning, and the clinic could refrigerate medicines and vaccines, dramatically improving healthcare. "We used to feel left behind," the schoolteacher, Mr. Anand, told Aadir during a visit to the school. "Now, we can give our children the education they deserve."

Aadir maintained a strong partnership with the village. Through regular visits and updates, EcoInnovate ensured that the systems were maintained and the community continued to benefit from the technology. "This is just the beginning," Aadir reiterated during a follow-up meeting with the village leaders. "Together, we can bring clean and affordable energy to communities around the world, ensuring a brighter and more sustainable future for all." His words, once just a promise, were now a reality, lighting up lives one village at a time. As he left the village, the glow from the solar-powered lights was a beacon of hope—not just for that village but for other communities waiting for their dawn.

• 81 •

TWENTY-FIVE

The conference room at EcoInnovate's headquarters was dimly lit, the glow from a large screen illuminating concerned faces as footage of recent natural disasters played. Devastating hurricanes, earthquakes, and floods were wreaking havoc across the globe, leaving behind a trail of destruction.

Aadir, seated at the head of the table, paused the footage, turning to address his team. The weight of their task was palpable in his serious tone. "We can't prevent natural disasters, but we can mitigate their impact," he stated firmly. "Our goal is to help vulnerable communities prepare for and respond to these disasters more effectively." The team leaned in, ready to tackle the challenge. Ideas began to flow, focusing on leveraging technology to build disaster resilience.

"Let's think about early warning systems first," suggested Vadish, the lead engineer. "If we can improve the accuracy and speed of alerts, it could give people more time to evacuate." The team discussed integrating advanced seismic sensors with a networked system that utilized satellite data to enhance predictive capabilities. The idea was to create an algorithm that could analyze shifts in tectonic plates and oceanic conditions to predict tsunamis and major storms with greater accuracy. Paravi chimed in with a proposal for disaster-resistant infrastructure. "We need to consider how buildings can withstand these events. I'm thinking modular, flexible designs that absorb shocks rather than resist them."

Aadir knew that technology alone wouldn't be enough; they needed strong partnerships on the ground. "We must collaborate with local governments and community leaders to ensure these technologies are implemented effectively," he noted. To this end, EcoInnovate hosted workshops with local officials and emergency responders, sharing knowledge and resources to foster a collaborative approach to disaster preparedness. They discussed site-specific challenges and adapted their technologies to meet these needs, ensuring local buy-in and effectiveness.

The first prototype of their tsunami warning system was installed in a small coastal community prone to earthquakes. The system included underwater pressure sensors linked to satellite communications that sent data directly to local emergency services and residents' mobile devices. During a controlled test, the system successfully detected simulated abnormal wave patterns and issued alerts within minutes, significantly faster than existing systems. The community's feedback was overwhelmingly positive, with local leaders expressing gratitude for the sense of security the system provided.

Encouraged by the success of their pilot projects, EcoInnovate planned to expand their initiatives. Aadir outlined a vision for a network of sensors along vulnerable coastlines worldwide and stressed the importance of ongoing support and maintenance to ensure the longevity of these systems.

"Our work isn't just about innovation for innovation's sake," Aadir remarked. "It's about real-world impact, about making a tangible difference in people's lives when they need it most." The team's commitment to enhancing disaster resilience was more than just a professional mission; it was a moral imperative to use their skills and resources to protect and empower those facing the greatest risks.As Aadir was leaving, Vadish pounded on him in excitement , "Hey! Soon to be the groom should be at home, resting for tomorrow's special day". Aadir could not help but blush and imagine Snigdha in the bridal look.While they both left the conference room, Aadir reminded Vadish to be at the venue before time the next day.

TWENTY-SIX

The sun had barely risen when the household stirred with the excitement of Snigdha and Aadir's wedding day. The courtyard was adorned with marigold garlands and strings of fairy lights, creating a vibrant and festive atmosphere. Women dressed in bright saris moved gracefully, their bangles clinking softly as they prepared for the grand event.

In Snigdha's room, the air was thick with the scent of jasmine and sandalwood. She sat in front of a mirror, her lehenga a rich crimson adorned with intricate gold embroidery. Her mother, Mrs. Bakshi, fussed over her jewelry, adjusting the maang tikka that rested elegantly on her forehead. "Snigdha, you look like a princess," her mother said, tears welling up in her eyes. "Ma, don't cry now, or you'll make me cry too," Snigdha replied, trying to keep her own emotions in check. Her best friend, Kashvi, handed her a tissue and said, "Come on, Snigdha, we can't have the bride with smudged makeup!" Downstairs, the groom's procession, or baraat, was about to arrive.

Aadir, dressed in a golden sherwani and a matching safa, sat atop a white horse, looking every bit the regal groom. His friends and family danced around him to the beat of the dhol, their energy infectious. "Are you ready, Aadir?" his best friend, Vadish shouted over the music. Aadir laughed, his nervousness dissolving in the joyous chaos. "Ready as I'll ever be," he shouted back. The baraat reached the entrance of Snigdha's house, where they were greeted by her family. A playful moment ensued as Mrs. Bakshi tried to feed Aadir a spoonful of honey, but he pretended to refuse, much to everyone's amusement.

Inside, the mandap was set up with traditional decorations of banana leaves and mango leaves, symbolizing prosperity and happiness. The sacred fire in the center awaited the couple. As Snigdha was escorted to the mandap, a hush fell over the gathering. The priest began chanting the mantras, their ancient words filling the air with solemnity and tradition. The couple exchanged garlands in the jaimala ceremony, laughter bubbling up as Snigdha's cousins tried to lift her off her feet to avoid the garland . Their friends and family cheered, capturing the moment on their phones. Snigdha was in love head over heels, ahe asked her cousins to put her down as she did not want anyone to tease Aadir.

"Don't make it too easy for him, Snigdha!" Kashvi teased. As the pheras began, Snigdha and Aadir circled the sacred fire seven times, promising to love and cherish each other for seven lifetimes. The priest recited the vows, and the couple repeated after him, their voices steady and full of commitment. In the final ritual, the sindoor was applied and the mangalsutra tied around Snigdha's neck. Aadir's hands were gentle but firm, his eyes locking with hers in a moment of shared understanding and love. The ceremony concluded with a chorus of congratulations and blessings. The newlyweds touched the feet of their elders, seeking their blessings. The atmosphere was filled with laughter, tears, and the ringing of bells, signaling the auspicious union.

Later, during the reception, the couple mingled with guests, their smiles never fading. The evening was a blend of dance, music, and sumptuous food. Aadir's parents performed a graceful dance number, and Snigdha's father gave a heartfelt speech that left many in tears. "To Snigdha and Aadir," he said, raising a toast. "May your life together be filled with love, laughter, and endless happiness." As the night drew to a close, Snigdha and Aadir finally had a moment to themselves.

Sitting under a canopy of stars, they reflected on the day's events. "Can you believe we're finally married?" Snigdha asked, resting her head on Aadir's shoulder. "It's surreal," he replied, his voice soft. "But

I couldn't be happier." They sat in comfortable silence, the weight of the day's traditions giving way to the lightness of their shared future. The festivities might have ended, but their journey together had just begun.

TWENTY-SEVEN

Both Snigdha and Aadir returned to work , soon after the wedding. While being in the newly-wed phase of life , they both knew their commitment to their work is the priority.

In the expansive conference room filled with industry leaders and policymakers, Aadir stood at the podium, ready to challenge the entrenched norms of production and consumption. The audience, a blend of skeptics and enthusiasts, waited for him to outline a vision that could potentially reshape industries.

"The linear 'take-make-dispose' model is reaching its limits," Aadir began, his voice steady and convincing. "We are faced with dwindling resources and escalating waste, signaling the urgent need for a shift to a circular economy where nothing is wasted and everything is reused." He paused, allowing the gravity of his words to sink in before continuing. "In a circular economy, we don't just use items and throw them away. Instead, we design them to be used again, repurposed, or recycled, infinitely."

The scene shifted to EcoInnovate's research facility, where Aadir and Vadish, his lead engineer, walked through a lab filled with prototypes and equipment. They stopped in front of a device that looked promising for electronic waste management. "Here's where we can make a tangible impact," Vadish pointed out, gesturing to the device. "This is a prototype for our new closed-loop recycling system designed specifically for e-waste. It can disassemble electronic devices to extract and reuse valuable materials like copper and gold."

As they discussed, Vadish detailed their approach to product design that facilitated recycling: "We're integrating modular designs that make it easier to repair or upgrade components instead of replacing the entire device. Additionally, we use materials that are easier to recycle, reducing the need for virgin resources and decreasing our environmental footprint."

Back at the conference, Aadir used these points to emphasize the need for collaborative efforts across industries. "To truly implement a circular economy, we need not only innovation but also supportive policies and a framework that incentivizes companies to make sustainable choices," he said. He proposed partnerships between private and public sectors to develop standards and regulations that encourage circular practices, such as extended producer responsibility and incentives for using recycled materials.

Concluding his presentation, Aadir outlined the broader benefits of adopting circular economy principles. "By reducing waste, we conserve resources and energy, lower pollution levels, and create new business opportunities through innovative recycling technologies and sustainable products," he explained. The audience, now more engaged, began a lively Q&A session, probing the feasibility and scalability of the proposed solutions.

Aadir and his team felt a renewed sense of purpose. They knew challenges lay ahead but remained committed to pioneering a sustainable future. EcoInnovate's initiatives had started small but had the potential to catalyze significant changes in how businesses and consumers view and utilize resources. Their work, Aadir believed, was not just about technological innovation but about fostering a cultural shift towards sustainability—a shift that would ensure prosperity and environmental health for future generations.

TWENTY-EIGHT

The hustle of urban life buzzed below the large windows of the boardroom where Aadir and several key representatives from leading transportation companies were convened. The cityscape stretched out, a visual testament to the urgency of their meeting.

As the group settled, Aadir took the lead, his voice carrying both concern and determination. "We're at a critical juncture," he began, eyeing the gathered executives. "Our transportation networks, as they stand, contribute significantly to global emissions. We have the opportunity—and responsibility—to pivot towards more sustainable practices." The room nodded in agreement, the gravity of the issue hanging over them like the smog outside.

The conversation shifted towards solutions. "Let's consider electric vehicles (EVs), hydrogen fuel cells, and sustainable biofuels," suggested Aadir. "Each of these technologies holds the potential to drastically cut emissions and should be integral to our strategy." An executive from a leading EV manufacturer added, "Electric vehicles are indeed promising, especially for city environments. However, the real challenge lies in infrastructure. Without adequate charging stations, even the best EVs are not practical for consumers." Aadir acknowledged this, proposing a collaborative approach. "What if we work together to roll out a network of charging stations? We could strategically place them in residential and commercial areas to ensure wide accessibility.

"The discussion took a concrete turn when the topic of public transportation came up. "We're also looking at electric buses powered by renewable energy," Aadir revealed. "These could serve as a clean, efficient backbone for urban transit." One of the public transportation officials chimed in, excitedly: "That's a game-changer. It not only lowers emissions but also improves air quality for our cities. What's the feasibility of rolling out a fleet in the next two years?" Aadir responded, "It's highly feasible. With your cooperation, we can pilot a program in select cities, measure the impact, and adjust our strategy accordingly."

A civil engineer among the group highlighted the need for additional infrastructure. "Beyond charging stations, we should consider the broader ecosystem—bike lanes, pedestrian paths, and even incentives for carpooling and public transit use can shift public behavior towards more sustainable options." Aadir agreed, noting, "True sustainability in transportation isn't just about the technology—it's about creating an environment that encourages its use. We need to ensure our cities are not just equipped but also conducive to green transportation."

The group had outlined a roadmap for integrating green transportation solutions. Aadir concluded, "This is more than just a business opportunity; it's our chance to lead by example, to show that sustainable transportation is not only viable but beneficial for all." The executives left the room energized, ready to take on the challenge of transforming the transportation landscape. Aadir's vision of cleaner, more efficient cities felt a step closer to reality, spurred on by innovation and collaborative effort.

TWENTY-NINE

In the heart of a busy city, a group of dedicated experts gathered in a conference room lined with maps pinpointing the world's water-stressed regions. The air was thick with determination as Aadir convened the meeting with water sector specialists, environmental engineers, and policy makers. The issue at hand was critical: global water scarcity.

Aadir opened the discussion with a clear and pressing statement: "Water scarcity affects billions and is exacerbated by climate change and population growth. We have the technology and knowledge to mitigate this issue; it's time we turn our focus to practical solutions." Around the room, heads nodded in agreement. The group was a mix of technical experts and strategic thinkers, each ready to contribute their insights.

The conversation shifted to potential technologies that could be harnessed to combat water scarcity. "Let's talk about rainwater harvesting systems," suggested Aadir. "Such systems could be crucial in regions where rainfall is infrequent and unpredictable." A hydrologist responded, "Absolutely, and when combined with water-efficient irrigation techniques, the impact could be significant. We can design systems that collect rainwater and use it during dry spells, reducing dependence on shrinking freshwater sources." The group also discussed the potential of desalination technologies. An engineer from the team added, "While desalination is energy-intensive, advances in solar energy could make it more viable. We can set up pilot projects in coastal regions where seawater is abundant but fresh water is scarce."

One of the standout ideas was the development of a smart irrigation system. "Using sensors and data analytics, we can precisely control the amount of water used in agriculture," explained Aadir. "This not only conserves water but also boosts crop yields by applying the right amount of water at the right time." The agricultural specialist in the room emphasized, "This approach can revolutionize farming in arid areas. It's crucial we get the local farming communities on board early to tailor the systems to their specific needs and conditions."

A vital component of their strategy involved community engagement. "Education is key," a policy advisor remarked. "We need to ensure that every household understands the importance of water conservation and how they can help save water daily." Aadir agreed, outlining a plan for community workshops and informational campaigns, "We'll collaborate with local schools and community centers to spread awareness and teach water-saving techniques that can be implemented at home."

The group agreed on a multi-pronged strategy to address water scarcity. Aadir summed up, "Our commitment to these initiatives must be unwavering. We are not just solving a problem; we are safeguarding our future." The team left the room energized, ready to tackle the challenges ahead. With a clear plan and a collaborative spirit, they were poised to make significant strides in water conservation, ensuring that communities worldwide have access to the vital resource of water.

THIRTY

Within the warm embrace of a rural village, beneath the expansive shade of an ancient tree, Aadir and a group of local community leaders gathered to discuss the empowerment of their community. The air was vibrant with the sounds of children playing nearby, infusing the meeting with a sense of hope and the urgency of the future at stake.

Aadir opened the meeting with a heartfelt address to the assembled leaders. "Empowerment starts with having a voice," he began. "It's about making sure that every decision reflects the needs and aspirations of its people. EcoInnovate is here not just to support but to facilitate a framework where you can lead your own development." The community leaders, a diverse group of men and women respected for their wisdom and dedication, listened intently. They represented various facets of village life—from education and healthcare to local business and traditional authorities.

The group engaged in a lively brainstorming session. Ideas flowed freely, focusing on sustainable, community-driven projects. "What about vocational training centers?" suggested one leader. "If we could train our youth in skills like carpentry, sewing, and technology, it could open up new opportunities for employment and self-reliance." Another leader brought up the idea of microfinance initiatives. "Access to small loans could empower our entrepreneurs, especially women, to start and grow their businesses. This financial boost could elevate entire families out of poverty," she explained.

As discussions continued, the idea of a community-owned solar cooperative took center stage. "Electricity is a catalyst for development," Aadir noted. "A solar cooperative could not only light up homes but also power small businesses and even charge community batteries." The group discussed how such a cooperative would work. It would involve training local residents to install and maintain solar panels, effectively creating jobs and transferring valuable skills to the community. Excess energy could be sold back to the grid, generating a steady income for the cooperative. "We can use the revenue to fund other community projects," a young leader added, his voice full of enthusiasm. "It could fund scholarships for our children or healthcare services for the elderly."

Ensuring the sustainability of these initiatives was a key topic. "It's essential that these projects are led by you, managed by you, and directly benefit all of you," Aadir emphasized. "Community-driven development is the most sustainable model because it builds capacity, not dependency." The community leaders agreed to establish a local committee to oversee the implementation of these initiatives. This committee would include representatives from various segments of the community to ensure a broad and inclusive approach.

While the meeting apprached to an end, the air was thick with a renewed sense of purpose and possibility. Aadir concluded, "Today, we've laid the groundwork for a transformative journey. Together, we will build a future where empowerment and equity light every path." The community leaders stood together, their faces bright with determination and hope, ready to lead their community towards a more empowered and equitable tomorrow. With the partnership of EcoInnovate, they were set to embark on a journey of lasting change.

THIRTY-ONE

In a brightly lit classroom adorned with vibrant educational posters, Aadir met with a diverse group of educators and community leaders. The classroom buzzed with the palpable enthusiasm of students engaged in learning, their desks cluttered with notebooks and educational tools. At the front, a chalkboard displayed complex mathematical equations and scientific diagrams, setting the scene for a discussion about transforming education.

Aadir stood at the front of the room, his eyes sweeping over the gathered individuals, each committed to the cause of education. "Today, we're here to tackle a critical challenge," he began earnestly. "Education is more than just learning; it's a gateway to personal and communal upliftment. At EcoInnovate, we are committed to ensuring that this gateway remains open to everyone, especially those in underserved communities." The group nodded, their faces a mixture of resolve and anticipation. They represented various facets of the educational spectrum, from seasoned teachers to nonprofit leaders, each bringing a unique perspective on overcoming educational barriers.

The meeting transitioned into a brainstorming session. Ideas flowed, each suggesting innovative ways to enhance educational access and quality. "One of our biggest challenges is infrastructure," one educator pointed out. "Many schools in remote areas lack even the basic facilities that are often taken for granted elsewhere." Aadir responded, "Let's consider how we can improve school infrastructures with sustainable materials and designs. Additionally, incorporating green spaces and renewable energy sources can create a healthier, more inviting learning environment." Discussion then turned to the importance of teacher training. "Investing in our teachers is investing in our future," a school principal said. "We need robust training programs that not only cover subject matter expertise but also teaching strategies that adapt to the diverse needs of students."

One of the key initiatives that emerged from the discussions was the development of digital learning platforms. "These platforms can bridge the gap between urban and rural education by providing remote communities access to quality educational content," explained a tech specialist in the group. Aadir elaborated on the vision, "Imagine a platform that offers everything from video lessons and interactive quizzes to virtual labs for science students. Such resources would be invaluable in areas where educational materials are scarce."

As the group discussed the logistics of digital platforms, a community leader emphasized inclusivity. "We need to ensure these platforms are accessible to all students. This means they should be usable on basic mobile phones and available in multiple languages." Aadir agreed wholeheartedly. "Our goal is to make education as inclusive as possible. We'll work with local communities to translate content and make it culturally relevant, ensuring it resonates with the students."

There was a shared sense of commitment to turning their ideas into action. Aadir concluded, "This is the beginning of a transformative journey. With your expertise and collaboration, we can dismantle the barriers to education and build a foundation that nurtures every student's potential." The educators and community leaders left the meeting energized, ready to collaborate and innovate. Under Aadir's leadership, EcoInnovate was set to spearhead efforts that would not only promote education but also empower communities, making 'Education for All' a tangible reality.

THIRTY-TWO

Inside the community center, draped with vibrant banners and powerful slogans promoting women's rights, Aadir met with an assembly of determined women's rights activists and community leaders. The air was charged with a shared commitment to fostering gender equality and the palpable urgency of the need for action.

Aadir opened the meeting with a strong affirmation of EcoInnovate's mission. "Empowering women is not just a moral imperative; it's a foundational element for sustainable development," he declared. "When women thrive, their communities flourish along with them. Our goal at EcoInnovate is to ensure that women have the tools they need to succeed." Nods of agreement met his statement, reinforcing the common ground shared by everyone in the room. The walls, adorned with posters of influential women leaders from around the world, served as a reminder of the potential impact of their work.

The group delved into a brainstorming session, each member eager to contribute their insights and experiences. "One of the most significant barriers is access to economic resources," noted a community leader. "We need to create pathways for women to be economically independent and resilient." From this discussion, the idea of a microfinance program took shape. Aadir listened intently as a financial expert explained, "Microfinance can be a powerful tool for women's empowerment. By providing small loans to women entrepreneurs, we enable them to start and grow businesses, which leads to financial independence and community development."

Attention then turned towards the development of leadership programs. "We need more than just economic initiatives; we need to cultivate leadership," argued a seasoned activist. "Training and mentorship programs can equip women with the skills necessary to lead in their communities and beyond." Aadir was quick to sketch out a plan. "Let's design a leadership curriculum that includes practical skills like negotiation, public speaking, and strategic planning, tailored specifically for women."

Recognizing the power of advocacy, the group discussed launching campaigns to challenge and change societal norms. "We need to address the root causes of inequality, which means changing how society views gender roles," mentioned a social worker involved in gender studies. "We'll create awareness campaigns that not only educate but also inspire action at all levels of society," Aadir responded. "These will highlight successful women and their stories to inspire others and show that change is possible."

"We are not just discussing policies; we are crafting a movement that will empower women across all sectors," Aadir said, capturing the collective sentiment of the group. He continued, "With these initiatives, from microfinance to leadership training and advocacy, we can create comprehensive support systems that empower women to achieve their full potential." The women left the meeting invigorated, ready to take the necessary steps to turn their plans into reality. Under Aadir's leadership, EcoInnovate was poised to be a catalyst for change, driving efforts that would not only support women but also propagate far-reaching impacts on global sustainable development.

THIRTY-THREE

The busy clinic, where the air was filled with the aroma of antiseptics and the sound of patients' voices, Aadir convened a meeting with a diverse group of healthcare professionals and community health workers. The atmosphere was one of shared determination to address the pressing issue of health inequality.

Aadir commenced the meeting with a firm affirmation of EcoInnovate's commitment to health equity. "Access to healthcare is not just a luxury; it's a basic human right," he emphasized. "Our goal is to ensure that every individual, regardless of their circumstances, has access to quality healthcare services." The room resonated with murmurs of agreement, underscoring the unanimous belief in the significance of their mission. The walls, adorned with posters promoting health awareness and prevention, served as a visual reminder of the importance of their work.

The group delved into a spirited brainstorming session, each member contributing their expertise and insights. "We need to bring healthcare services directly to the communities that need them the most," proposed a community health worker. "Mobile clinics can bridge the gap and provide essential care to underserved populations." Aadir nodded in agreement, recognizing the practicality and effectiveness of the suggestion. "Mobile clinics will allow us to reach remote areas and provide primary healthcare services to those who would otherwise go without."

Turning their attention to technological solutions, the group discussed the potential of telemedicine. "Telemedicine can revolutionize healthcare delivery, especially in rural and remote areas," remarked a technology enthusiast. "By leveraging digital platforms, we can connect patients with healthcare providers and specialists without the need for travel." Aadir seized upon the idea, envisioning a future where distance would no longer be a barrier to healthcare access. "Let's develop telemedicine programs that provide remote consultations, diagnostic services, and health education to communities in need."

Recognizing the importance of local empowerment, the group explored the concept of community health worker training. "Local residents are often the first point of contact for healthcare in their communities," noted a seasoned healthcare professional. "By equipping them with the necessary skills and knowledge, we can strengthen the healthcare system from within." Aadir wholeheartedly supported the idea. "Let's develop a comprehensive training program that empowers community health workers to provide essential healthcare services, promote preventive care, and advocate for the health needs of their communities."

The discussion then shifted towards addressing the root causes of health disparities. "Health outcomes are influenced by a multitude of factors, including poverty, education, and access to clean water and sanitation," highlighted a public health expert. Aadir nodded thoughtfully. "We must take a holistic approach to health and well-being, addressing not just the symptoms but also the underlying social determinants."

When the meeting was concluded, there was a palpable sense of solidarity and commitment among the participants. "Together, we can make a difference in the lives of countless individuals," Aadir affirmed. "Let's work tirelessly to ensure that everyone has access to the healthcare they need to lead healthy and fulfilling lives." With renewed determination, the group dispersed, each member ready to play their part in the collective effort to promote health and well-being for all. Under Aadir's leadership, EcoInnovate was poised to be a catalyst for change, driving initiatives that would not only improve health outcomes but also contribute to the realization of a more equitable and sustainable world.

THIRTY-FOUR

Through the EcoInnovate's mission to create a more equitable and sustainable future, Aadir convened a gathering of technology experts and community leaders. They met in a vibrant tech hub, where the incessant hum of electronics underscored the urgency of their discussion.

Addressing the diverse assembly, Aadir emphasized the pivotal role of technology in shaping the modern world. "Access to technology isn't just a luxury; it's a fundamental right," he asserted. "Our goal is to bridge the digital divide and empower individuals and communities to thrive in the digital age." The group's collective nod of agreement signaled a shared commitment to the cause. With a palpable sense of purpose, they embarked on a collaborative journey to explore innovative solutions for digital inclusion.

Enthusiastic ideas flooded the room as participants engaged in a spirited brainstorming session. "Community computer centers could serve as vital hubs for digital access and learning," proposed one community leader, igniting a wave of enthusiastic concurrence. Aadir seized upon the notion, recognizing its potential to democratize access to technology. "Community computer centers will not only provide access to digital tools but also foster a sense of community and collaboration," he affirmed.

Transitioning to education, the group delved into the importance of digital literacy. "Digital skills are the currency of the 21st century," emphasized a seasoned educator. "We must develop a comprehensive digital literacy curriculum to equip individuals of all ages with the skills they need to navigate the digital landscape."

Aadir echoed the sentiment, envisioning a curriculum that transcended barriers and empowered learners of all backgrounds. "Let's develop a curriculum that encompasses essential digital skills, from internet literacy to coding and online safety," he proposed.

Confronting the challenge of internet accessibility, the group explored solutions for affordable connectivity. "Internet access is a gateway to opportunity," underscored a telecommunications expert. "We must collaborate with service providers to develop affordable internet packages tailored to underserved communities." Aadir nodded in agreement, recognizing the pivotal role of internet access in leveling the playing field. "By ensuring that internet access is affordable and accessible to all, we can empower individuals to seize new opportunities for education, employment, and social participation."

In the end, a sense of solidarity pervaded the room. "Together, we can pave the way for a more inclusive and equitable digital future," Aadir affirmed. "Let's harness the power of technology to bridge divides and unlock new pathways to prosperity for all." With renewed determination, the participants dispersed, each committed to playing their part in the collective effort to promote digital inclusion. Under Aadir's leadership, EcoInnovate was poised to lead the charge in driving initiatives that would not only bridge the digital divide but also pave the way for a more equitable and sustainable future.

THIRTY-FIVE

In a testament to EcoInnovate's commitment to global cooperation, Aadir convened a diverse assembly of representatives from governments, NGOs, and international organizations. The meeting took place in a conference room adorned with flags from across the globe, symbolizing the diversity and unity of the participants.

Addressing the esteemed gathering, Aadir emphasized the urgency of global solidarity in addressing the world's most pressing challenges. "No single country or organization can tackle these challenges alone," he asserted. "It's only through united efforts and shared commitment that we can create a more sustainable and equitable world for all." The representatives nodded in agreement, recognizing the imperative of collective action in addressing complex global issues. With a spirit of collaboration and determination, they embarked on a journey to explore avenues for fostering greater international solidarity.

Diverse perspectives and ideas permeated the room as participants engaged in a lively brainstorming session. "Joint research projects could leverage the expertise of diverse stakeholders to develop innovative solutions," suggested a representative from an international research institute, sparking enthusiastic discussion. Aadir seized upon the suggestion, recognizing the potential of collaborative research in driving progress. "Let's establish partnerships for joint research initiatives that harness the collective knowledge and resources of our global community," he proposed, eliciting nods of agreement from the group.

Transitioning to climate action, the group delved into the imperative of supporting vulnerable communities in adapting to climate change. "Climate change is a global challenge that requires a global response," emphasized a representative from a developing country. "We must establish a global climate fund to provide support for adaptation and mitigation efforts in the most vulnerable regions." Aadir echoed the sentiment, acknowledging the disproportionate impact of climate change on the world's most vulnerable communities. "Let's mobilize resources and expertise to establish a global climate fund that ensures no one is left behind in the transition to a sustainable future," he affirmed.

Confronting the complexities of international cooperation, the group explored strategies for overcoming barriers and fostering greater collaboration. "We must strengthen partnerships and build bridges between nations and sectors," remarked a seasoned diplomat. "By fostering trust and mutual respect, we can overcome differences and work together towards common goals." Aadir nodded in agreement, recognizing the importance of building relationships based on trust and mutual understanding. "Let's forge ahead with renewed determination and solidarity," he urged. "Together, we can overcome challenges and build a more just, peaceful, and sustainable world for generations to come."

While the day came to the dawn, a palpable sense of solidarity pervaded the room. "In unity, there is strength," affirmed Aadir, his voice resolute. "Let's continue to work together, hand in hand, to create a future where every individual and community can thrive." With a renewed sense of purpose and commitment, the representatives dispersed, each carrying with them the shared vision of a more sustainable and equitable world. Under Aadir's leadership, EcoInnovate was poised to play a pivotal role in fostering global solidarity and driving collective action towards a brighter future.

THIRTY-SIX

Aadir stood before a packed auditorium, the stage adorned with banners celebrating EcoInnovate's journey. It was a momentous occasion, marking the end of an era and the beginning of a new chapter in the company's legacy. "We started this journey with a vision," Aadir began, his voice filled with emotion. "A vision of a world where innovation drives sustainability, where collaboration fosters progress, and where every individual has the opportunity to thrive."

The audience listened intently, reflecting on the challenges overcome and the milestones achieved over the years. From pioneering technologies to empowering communities, EcoInnovate had left an indelible mark on the world. "But our journey was not without its challenges," Aadir continued, his voice tinged with nostalgia. "We faced skeptics and naysayers, setbacks and failures. But through it all, we remained steadfast in our commitment to creating a better world." As Aadir spoke, images flashed on the screen behind him – of groundbreaking innovations, of empowered communities, of resilient ecosystems restored to their former glory. Each image was a testament to the company's impact and the power of collective action. "But our journey does not end here," Aadir declared, his voice ringing with determination. "As we close this chapter, we look to the future with hope and optimism. We must continue to push the boundaries of innovation, to challenge the status quo, and to build a more sustainable and equitable future for all." The audience erupted into applause, a thunderous roar of appreciation and gratitude.

For Aadir and his team, it was a moment of validation – a reaffirmation of their purpose and their impact on the world. As the applause died down, Aadir turned to his colleagues, his eyes shining with pride. "I am deeply grateful to each and every one of you," he said, his voice choked with emotion. "Together, we have achieved the impossible, and our legacy will endure for generations to come." Tears welled up in the eyes of the team members, a mixture of sadness at the end of an era and pride in their collective accomplishments. They embraced each other, knowing that their journey was far from over – that the spirit of EcoInnovate would live on in the hearts and minds of all who had been touched by its impact. And as they looked to the future, they knew that no matter what challenges lay ahead, they would face them with the same determination, resilience, and unwavering commitment to creating a better world.The audience noticed as Aadir and Snigdha exchanged glimpses with eyes full of tears and hearts full of gratitude. They could feel that Snigdha's and Aadir's love knew no bounds.

For in the end, it was not just about the technologies they had developed or the projects they had undertaken – it was about the people whose lives they had touched, the communities they had empowered, and the legacy they had built together.

Epilogue

Aadir was standing at the edge of his hometown, the familiar sights and sounds stirred memories long forgotten. The bustling streets, the vibrant markets, the smell of spices in the air – it was as if time had stood still, preserving the essence of his childhood. As he walked through the narrow lanes, Aadir felt a sense of nostalgia wash over him. He passed by the small shop where he used to buy sweets with his pocket money, the park where he played cricket with his friends, the school where he first dreamed of changing the world. But as he wandered through the streets of his hometown, Aadir realized that he was no longer the same person who had left all those years ago. He had grown and changed, shaped by his experiences and driven by his passion to make a difference in the world. As he reflected on his journey, Aadir couldn't help but feel a sense of pride in how far he had come. From being the odd one out, the dreamer who dared to challenge convention, he had forged his own path and built something truly remarkable – EcoInnovate. But more than the accolades and achievements, Aadir realized that his greatest strength had always been his ability to see the world differently, to think outside the box, to embrace change and uncertainty with courage and conviction.

As he visited his old neighborhood, Aadir couldn't help but smile as he remembered the doubters and skeptics who had once dismissed his ideas as foolish and impractical. They had underestimated him, underestimated his determination to prove them wrong and to show the world what was possible. But as Aadir walked through the streets of his hometown, he realized that it wasn't about proving anyone wrong – it was about staying true to himself, to his values, to his vision for a better world. And in doing so, he had inspired others to follow in his footsteps, to dream big and to never give up on their dreams. As the sun began to set, casting a warm glow over the horizon, Aadir found himself standing at the edge of a cliff overlooking the town. Below him, he could see the lights twinkling in the distance, a reminder of the lives he had touched and the impact he had made. In that moment, Aadir felt a profound sense of gratitude – for the opportunities he had been given, for the people who had supported him, for the journey that had brought him to this place.

And as he looked out at the world stretching out before him, he knew that his work was far from over – that there were still challenges to overcome, dreams to pursue, and lives to change. But no matter what the future held, Aadir knew one thing for certain – he would always carry with him the lessons he had learned, the memories he had made, and the love he had for his hometown. He realised , it was not about the destination – it was about the journey, the people, and the moments that had shaped him into the person he had become. And as he stood there, surrounded by the beauty of his hometown, Aadir couldn't help but feel a sense of peace and contentment wash over him, knowing that he had found his place in the world – a place where he belonged, a place where he could make a difference, a place he could always call home.

About The Author

Sneha Jain has made significant strides in the literary world at just 23 years old. A world record holder recognized as an "Aspiring Author 2021" by Bravo International Book of Records, Sneha also boasts a place in the India Book of Records for her acclaimed second book, "She - The Withered Flower." Her impressive achievements have earned her the prestigious Bharat Vibhushan Award in 2023. Balancing her writing career with her academic pursuits, Sneha is currently completing her Masters in English. Her debut book, "The Visionary Lights from a Dark Mind," launched at the age of 19, marked the beginning of her journey as an author. Since then, she has published several notable works, including "She - The Withered Flower," a powerful narrative on women's empowerment, "The Jewels of Elegance," a patriotic tribute to India, "The Wind and the Grit," a collection of poems on natural elements, "Be the First You," a motivational guide and 'Threads of life : Stories Woven from Ordinary Moments" , a short story anthology. All her books are globally available on Amazon. Sneha's dedication to her craft has been recognized with numerous awards.Sneha continues to inspire and motivate through her writing, particularly with themes of women empowerment. She believes in expressing the realities of the world through her words, encouraging everyone to voice their opinions and stay true to themselves. Her motto, "Always be the first you instead of trying to be the next them," resonates deeply in all her works.

"A Lone Trailblazer" marks Sneha's first venture into contemporary fiction, promising to leave readers inspired and reflective of the transformative power of perseverance, innovation, and collaboration.